The Document within the Walls
The Romance of Bassani

The Document within the Walls
The Romance of Bassani

Guia Risari

*t*roubador

Published by
Troubador Publishing Ltd
12 Manor Walk, Coventry Road
Market Harborough
Leics LE16 9BP, UK
Tel: (+44) 1858 469898
Fax: (+44) 1858 431649
Email: troubador@compuserve.com

in association with

 Hull Italian Texts
Department of Italian
University of Hull
Hull HU6 7RX
Email: a.d.thompson@italian.hull.ac.uk

Series Editor
Professor A. D. Thompson
University of Hull, UK

ISBN 1 899293 66 3

Cover design taken from a map showing Ferrara at the beginning of the 19th century.

Typesetting: Troubador Publishing Ltd, Market Harborough, UK
Printed and bound by Selwood Printing Ltd, UK

Contents

Acknowledgements   vii

INTRODUCTION   ix

1.   **THE ROMANCE OF HISTORY**   1
         1. The Life and the Romance   1
         2. The History of the Romance   3
         3. A Historical Narrative   4

2.   **BENEVOLENCE AND BETRAYAL**   7
         1. The myth of the Good Italian   8
         2. The Counter-myth of the Italian Diffidence   10
         3. Ferrara: a Microcosm of Fascism   12

3.   **THE DOCUMENT BY BASSANI**   15
         1. Reading through History   15
         2. A Literary Strategy   21
         3. The Shaping of Memory   25

         Conclusion   29

         Notes   31

         Bibliography   39

HULL ITALIAN TEXTS

Acknowledgements

If I have a long list of people to thank, as my work is the result not only of my solitary reading and pondering over texts, but also of discussions and the exchange of ideas.

First, I would like to thank the Centre for Jewish Studies of the University of Leeds for the critical frame given to me during my study. I thank all members of staff who have actively participated, and the lecturers for the interesting seminars. In particular, I would like to thank Professor Griselda Pollock for the challenging debates. Thanks are also due to Doctor Eva Frojmovic, whose suggestions and support have been crucial.

A special commendation should be made to Doctor Simon Lowy, who has provided me with an important background on Jewish thought and history (not to mention the delicious coffee breaks). I also thank Professor David Cesarani for his helpful criticism of my project. The historical contextualisation of my work has been, in great part, a response to his indications. I am especially grateful to Doctor Peter Fuller from the Department of Italian at Leeds. His encouragement and assistance have transformed the critical moments into pleasant hours.

Outside England, I must express my utmost appreciation to Professor Berel Lang for the discussions of philosophy and morals, which have reminded me of the inner reason for my study.

As well as the many people who have intellectually inspired me, I would like to thank the many who made my work practically possible. In this respect, I wish I could mention any single librarian of the Brotherton Library at Leeds. They faced my continual absent-mindness, recovering my books, my files and my precious library card, wherever they were hidden. I express my gratitude to the staff of the C.E.D.E.C., the Centre for Jewish Documentation of Milan. Although they had less time to experience my faults, experience them they did.

If the reader is able to penetrate into the meanderings of my language and, through it, into the quotations from Bassani, the blame should be put on Jane Dobson and Doctor Elisabeth Smith. They revised with a precise and sensitive touch my whole work.

Finally, I would like to confirm the "myth of the Good Italian", rendering a very special thanks to my family. My grandmother, my great-aunt and my mother, despite the distance, have been a supportive and affectionate presence. It has been at the familial 'round table' that I have developed my dialectic capacity. The main victim of it, however, is not my work, but my beloved Andrea, who has paid the dearest phone bills generated since the invention of this device. To my helpmate, therefore, I dedicate my study.

Guia Risari
September 1999

Introduction

My interest in the narrative of Bassani was born in England, thanks perhaps to the distance from my motherland and to the critical approach of the Centre for Jewish Studies of the University of Leeds. It was in this academic context that I first heard mention of Italian anti-Semitism and the inglorious side of the alleged 'myth of the Good Italian'. The seminar on this issue was held by Professor Paola Di Cori, and it provoked in me anger and vexation[1]. The subject of my philosophy thesis had already led me to the study of anti-Semitism, Nazi extermination of the Jews and the various forms of stereotype of 'the Jew'[2]. Nevertheless, not one of my sources had ever highlighted specifically the case of Italy. Paola Di Cori's seminar, however, sowed the seeds of suspicion and curiosity, which have slowly matured. In the meantime, Zygmund Bauman's analysis of the relationship between modernity and the holocaust have been most stimulating[3], and have framed the background of my study. Modernity appears as an epoch dominated by order, homogeneity and functionality. These characteristics reshaped the ancient prejudice against the Jews, identified now more than ever with the irredeemable 'Other', the Different *par excellence*. This has been essential for me in understanding that, contradicting the myth of the Good Italian, in Italy too there was a whole bureaucratic machinery working efficiently against the Jews. Hence the importance of recent historiography providing, by dint of dates, documentation and local testimonies, a new picture of Italian Fascism. If the argument denying a well accepted stereotype represents one side of my interest, the other is related to the actual process of bearing witness.

In studying the Holocaust literature, many critiques enlarge the meaning of witnessing and call into question the existence of a sharp distinction between 'objective' and 'subjective' records. Very important, in this respect, has been the reading of *Testimony: Crisis of Witnessing in Literature, Psychoanalysis and History*, by Shoshanna Felman and Dori Laub. The latter has especially shown the impossibility of being a direct recorder of "an event without witness", such as the Shoà. One can bear witness on three levels: as a witness of his/her own story; as witness of another's story; or as a witness of the process of witnessing itself[4]. This discourse, together with the studies problematizing the notion of representation, extends the frontiers of the Holocaust literature. James Young, for example, in *Writing and Rewriting the Holocaust*, points out clearly the impossibility of separating the historical from the literary truths. Writing on the Shoà has passed through many stages, from the first diaries, to the 'Hasidic Tale' by Jaffa Eliach, to the confessional poems of Sylvia Plath. If, in the beginning, this literature was made primarily of personal accounts and memoirs, it has progressively become a means for commemorating, interpreting and transforming the Event and other traumas. Finally, no narration is truer than another, as they all have a fictional and historical side. "Are historical tracts of the Holocaust less mediated by imagination, less troped and figured, or ultimately less interpretative that the fictions of the Holocaust? In what way do historians fictionalize and novelist historicize?", wonders Young[5].

It was while keeping these and other observations in my mind that I approached the *Romance of Ferrara* by Giorgio Bassani. Bassani is not the only Italian writer telling of the exclusion and the persecution of the Jews. Besides the well-known Primo Levi, there are also the accounts of Carlo Levi in 'The Watch' and of Curzio Malaparte in 'Kaputt'. Elsa Morante has quoted as the inspiration for her 'Story' the mass deportation of the Roman Jews. But Bassani is really the only one among them who has devoted all his narrative to descriptions of the Jews. For this reason, the persistence in his texts of a Jewish subject, a literary critic has defined Bassani the most important Italian-Jewish writer[6]. In Bassani's *Romanzo*, in fact, I have found the best literary anticipation of the historical debate on Italian anti-Semitism. Since his first stories, Bassani has underlined the sense of exclusion and the self-hatred of the assimilated Jews of Italy, or better, of the Italian microcosm of Ferrara. At the same time, in depicting the destructive reactions of his Jewish personages, Bassani records the trauma caused by the Racial Laws and the persecution. The degree of ambivalence of Bassani's Jews testifies at once the depth of their assimilation and the violence of the Christian rejection. Finally, the Romanzo is also a testimony to the author's effort to escape the trap of nostalgia. From this point of view, I disagree with those literary critics who, like Douglas Radcliff-Umsted, stress the consolatory character of Bassani's writing[7]. I do not think that Bassani's aim was to immortalise a lost world; rather, he has never left the past, feeling the danger of its illusions – hence Bassani's continual revision not only of his stories, but also of his political and moral positions. According to Marilyn Schneider, whose literary study on Bassani has been fundamental for me, "The author's role is thus to be a visionary leader – messiah or prophet – who evokes the 'sense of time' required for a difficult journey to moral worth"[8].

I consider my work as an enquiry into the question of Italian anti-Semitism and Jewish assimilation, made through the analysis of *The Romance of Ferrara* by Giorgio Bassani. In Chapter 1, 'The Romance of History', I have introduced the Italian writer, the structure of his *Romanzo* and its main theme, that is, the isolation of the assimilated Jew[9]. If Bassani's narrative dismisses the 'myth of the Good Italian', his declared historicism relates to the specific context of Ferrara. To these two issues, the deconstruction of the myth and the history of Ferrarese Jewry, I have dedicated Chapter 2, 'Benevolence and Betrayal'. The historical perspective hopefully casts a new light on the whole *Romanzo*. In the final chapter, 'The Document by Bassani', I have realised a close reading of the text, following mainly three aspects of this document: the historical, the literary and the personal.

What I would like to suggest, as a conclusion, is that the *Romanzo* should be considered, in its entirety, not as a mere collection of novels, but as a document examining many questions: the Italian betrayal and the Jewish assimilation; the persecution under Fascism; and the painful disenchantment of the victims. Finally, the *Romanzo*, being dominated by an overwhelming sense of separateness and enclosure, may well be seen as 'A Document Within the Walls'.

1   The Romance of History

Muore un'epoca l'altra è già qua
affatto nuova e
innocente
ma anche questa lo so non la
potrò vivere che girato
perennemente all'indietro a guardare
verso quella testé
finita
a tutto indifferente tranne a che
cosa davvero fosse la mia
vita di prima
chi sia io mai
stato

G. Bassani: 'Muore un'epoca'[10]

1.   The Life and the Romance

Bassani is an Italian writer, born in 1916 of an upper middle-class Jewish family from Ferrara. Although Bologna was the centre of his cultural life, Ferrara remained the place of his first affections and friendships as well as deep delusions. Perfectly integrated in the local environment, he was even a member of the G.U.F. (University Fascist Group) and collaborated with the Fascist *Il Corriere Padano*[11]. In 1938, the Racial Laws deprived the young, just like many characters of his novels, of the usual rights and leisure facilities. In the same year, he was called to teach literature at the Jewish School of Ferrara, where he was a brilliant and stimulating teacher[12]. In the meantime, he began his anti-fascist activity in the Resistance group called 'Partito d'Azione'. In the spring of 1943, he was

1

arrested as a Resistance member and spent three months in Ferrara's prison[13]. Liberated with the fall of Fascism, he fled with his family to Florence. They hid until the end of the war, managing to escape deportation. After the war, Bassani moved to Rome, where he started his career as a journalist and writer. Occasionally, he collaborated with some art directors as a scenographer.

In 1955, Bassani was among the founders and later the president of 'Italia Nostra', a cultural association devoted to protecting the cultural and natural heritage of the country[14].

Bassani's debut as a writer was in *Il Corriere Padano*. From 1935 to 1937 there appeared a series of short stories, where Bassani's fundamental vocation is already present. Anna Folli states, in particular, three important elements in the early Bassani: the love for literature, the close relation with the 'padanità' and his poetic of memory. Dominant in these brief writings, almost pictures, is the sense of exclusion, the senility of the characters and their evocative tendency.

The twenty year-old protagonist of 'Caduta dell'amicizia' (Loss of Friendship) confesses to himself his obsession with the past: "And when I had not yet perhaps begun to live (...) I was little by little won over by a fierce and desperate nostalgia. I walked with my head turned to the way already covered"[15].

In any case, the first stories of Bassani lacked an essential element of his narrative style, the historicism. It was thanks to this perspective that Bassani passed from F. to Ferrara, introducing the principle of realism in his work. Pier Paolo Pasolini considered this change the true beginning of Bassani's writing. "Before this, there was the prehistory of a man who persecuted, excluded and considered unworthy of living, could not, objectively, look reality straight in the face; and the being of a writer who institutionalised such conditions of impotence"[16]. Historicism came later and slowly, also due to the temporal and spatial distance from Ferrara and the crucial years of Fascism. It was in Rome that Bassani started writing the first stories published later as *Le cinque storie di Ferrara* (The Five Stories of Ferrara) (1956). A second version of them, *Le Storie ferraresi* (Ferrarese Stories) (1962), already contains some important changes. The generic and allusive elements were eliminated on behalf of a more detailed description. The places acquired their precise names; the time was supported by dates, transformed into a historical epoch. The third and final revision of the stories became the first section of a wider work, *Il Romanzo di Ferrara* (The Romance of Ferrara) (1978), a massive collection of stories and novels. This time the five stories are significantly entitled 'Dentro le mura' (Within the Walls), and a new consciousness seems to be gained by the author. That of being Jewish, that of having always been separated from the rest of the environment by means of an invisible barrier, later tragically evident.

A literary critic has defined the *Romanzo* as an 'epic poem'. Within the microcosm of Ferrara, in fact, are depicted the Jewish community, along with the Catholics, the bourgeois and the common people of Ferrara. In his opinion, the *Romanzo* is a choral testimony of the past[17].

If it is true that the *Romanzo* is a testimony, it seems to me that it is more individual than choral, more determined by specific political events than from an indefinite 'epos'. I would rather agree with Ada Neiger, who holds that the very subject of all Bassani's narrative is the 'marginal Jew'[18]. At the centre of the *Romanzo* there is the interrogation of the Diasporic Jew on his identity. The many protagonists of the *Romanzo* express a plurality of positions faced with the Jewish question. Many of them, being almost completely assimilated, had ignored the problem until that moment; few are the orthodox, while others apparently reject their Judaism. In fact, the majority of them are in a very ambiguous position, both desiring and mistrusting assimilation. Important is the constant, although discreet, presence of the narrator, whose awareness dismantles many illusions. What really emerges is the impossibility of taking a position without immediately becoming an outcast. Marginalisation, exile, solitude – eventually persecution and disappearance – seem to be the destiny for those who claim an identity and for those who are searching for it. Finally, the setting of the *Romanzo*, Ferrara, is represented as a communal prison, a ghetto which both encloses and excludes. In this sense, Anna Dolfi, one of the major Italian critics of Bassani, speaks of the 'diaphragm of the distance', as an original frame and an interpretative key for his narrative[19].

2.   The History of the Romance

All the writings in the *Romanzo* deal with the Jews of Ferrara before, during or immediately after the Fascist epoch. The last five years of the dictatorship, from 1938 to 1943, are particularly crucial. They appear again and again in Bassani's narrative not only as historical dates, but also as symbolic moments of sudden waking up, painful growth and disillusion. Over the five stories which constitute 'Within the Walls', four have at their centre a young Jewish male, serching for a self-definition and struggling against being assimilated into either the Jewish community or the local environment.

The first two stories treat the theme of problematic relationships between a Jewish man and a 'goyà'. In *Lidia Mantovani*, the working-class girl is left by the aristocratic David. Neither their sexual affair nor their child succeed in creating a real relationship. In *La passeggiata prima di cena* (The Walk before Dinner), Elias Corcos and Gemma Brondi face a similar situation, although within the legal sanction of marriage. The Jewish background and the rural Christian one do not conflict, but never enter into a fruitful communication.

Una lapide in via Mazzini (A Plaque in Via Mazzini) tells of the return of Geo Josz, the only survivor of the deported Ferrarese Jews. His strange behaviour and his final, mysterious disappearance express the radical alterity of Geo.

Diversity and isolation are also the issues of *Gli ultimi anni di Clelia Trotti* (The Last Years of Clelia Trotti). Here Bruno Lattes, facing the Racial Laws and the impossibility of accepting his Jewishness, seeks salvation in political commitment. Nonetheless, the socialist ideals of an old-fashioned teacher do not compensate for the loss.

The fifth story, *Una notte del '43* (A Night in 1943) presents the non-Jewish Pino

Barillari as the silent witness of fascist violence, the infamous massacre of Via Mazzini. The four novels that follow 'Within the Walls' also explore the problem of Jewish existence and survival in a hostile environment.

Gli occhiali d'oro (The Gold-rimmed Eyeglasses) parallels the exile of a Jewish adolescent after the Racial Laws and the exclusion of a homosexual, the otorhinolaryngologist Fadigati.

Il giardino dei Finzi-Contini (The Garden of the Finzi-Continis) depicts the life of voluntary marginalisation of an aristocratic Jewish family in Ferrara. Since they are estranged from the assimilated Jews, they show no suffering or surprise at the discriminatory policy of Fascism. But they will never be buried in the monumental family tomb, as they are all deported to Buchenwald.

Dietro la porta (Behind the Doo)] is apparently a novel of adolescence and its turmoils, whereas the deepest theme is once again that of being different, marginalised from an apparently homogeneous context.

Finally, *L'airone* (The Heron) is the suicidal one-day journey of a middle-aged man. Rescued from the Nazi-Fascist persecution by escaping to Switzerland, he can no longer adapt himself to his previous way of life. Everything, including his own persona, seems to be meaningless, unworthy.

The last part of the *Romanzo* is entitled *L'odore del fieno* (The Smell of Hay), and contains little stories, two tales, some brief sketches and some autobiographical notes. One of the latter, is *Laggiù in fondo al corridoio* (Way down at the End of the Corridor), where we find a confirmation of Bassani's early attachment to the past.

> "The past is not dead... it never dies. It moves away, to be sure: every moment. To recover the past is therefore possible. You must, nonetheless, if you truly desire to recover it, go down a kind of corridor that gets longer every minute. Down there, at the end of the distant, sunny point of convergence of the corridor's black walls, is life, as vivid and as palpitating as it was once, when it was produced in the first place"[20].

3. A Historical Narrative

From the literary point of view, Bassani was influenced by the elegiac style and the funereal poetry of Decadentism. Moreover, the prose of Proust, Joyce, Mann and James was the main source for a narrative which is dependent both on memory and history. In any case, Bassani is not only a scholar of literature. To the imperative to remember and recover the past, Bassani has devoted all his narrative work. He was, in fact, a historical witness of the rising of Fascism in Italy and, particularly, in the area of Ferrara. Moreover, he was informed by the values of the Resistance movement and by the historicism of Benedetto Croce. The Resistance offered to Bassani the ethical-political dimension of engagement. It showed to the young writer the importance of remembering past evil in order to safeguard and renew the present.

The Crocean historicism, for its part, gave to Bassani faith in historical continuity. If history had an inner meaning, then it was impossible to regard the past as useless or definitely bygone.

Bassani's vision of history is quite complex; it identifies neither with the simplicity of Neo-realism nor with the aridity of the chronicle[21]. Events, just as lives, are more mysterious; elude banal explications, and they also resist being reduced to just one voice. Another important teacher of Bassani was the art historian Roberto Longhi, whose lectures he had attended in the University of Bologna. In his studies of the Renaissance painters, Longhi had stressed the influence of any local environment on the various artistic currents. So, there is not one history of Renaissance painting; there are rather the stories of many areas of painting.

All these influences are present in the narrative of Bassani: the moral issue of the Resistance, the Crocean sense of history and the depiction of local realities deriving from Longhi.

Bassani's effort to recall a precise, historical reality does not exclude the use of a selective and transforming memory, which nevertheless always retains some elements of reality. In an interview, Bassani declared on the nature of his art: "My aim is to realise an art which does not expect any precedence over life, an art which is simply a mimesis of life"[22].

In according with the aspiration thus expressed, Bassani continued that his characters are not to be considered fictional creations, inanimate puppets. They are, on the contrary, true, flesh and blood persons, having independence from the author and their secrets. Perhaps this merging of fiction and reality can be described by saying that the writer's characters are fictionalised realities, arisen from his private universe. So the character Geo Josz, the survivor of *A Plaque in Via Mazzini*, was suggested to the author by the Ferrarese Eugenio Ravenna, who was in fact deported to Auschwitz and, like the fictional character, had severed all relations with the Jewish community.

The socialist school teacher who, in *The Last Year of Clelia Trotti*, is arrested and controlled by the Fascist police, is modelled upon the life of Alda Costa.

By the same token, the Finzi-Continis and the blond, attractive Micòl have some superficial analogies with the Ferrarese family of the Finzi-Magrinis and their daughter Giuliana.

Ferrara, then, is described with such topographical precision as to suggest a concrete universe, despite the inclusion of fictitious locations. A map of the villa and the garden of the Finzi-Continis has been placed in the first pages of the novel, as if it were a document of a real place. On the contrary, the place does not exist, although the map has been drawn by Bassani on the basis of some models of Renaissance villas.

Finally, historical events are included in the *Romanzo* as an essential background to events, without which all the plots would be empty and meaningless. The Racial Laws, the deportation, but also the earlier events of the Risorgimento and the emancipation should be considered as protagonists along with the actors playing in these stories. Sometimes the events are shown by a collection of details; sometimes they are announced by the psychological moods of the protagonists. Frequently, they are summarised in a line, perhaps in the final part. It happens also that the absence itself of explicit reference becomes the best expressive means, a sort of literary silence[23].

Some Marxist literary critics have interpreted the presence of the historical and fictional trends in Bassani's *Romanzo* as a contrast, due to the persistence in the writer of an elegiac literary tendency. The dualism of Bassani's writing is fed by both a critical and a mythical vision of the past, and its aim would be to transcend the historical reality. Hence, the individualism and the enigmatic characters of Bassani's protagonists[24].

A similar line follows the sharp analysis of Enzo Siciliano, who speaks of the failure of Bassani's historicism. The writer's vision of the past, in fact, derives from a personal wound and tends to crystallise the events. Bassani's historicism does not accept the dialectical solution of the past, since it wants to immortalise it. So it fails as a gnosiological tool to become rather a means of commemoration. "That is why – the critic concludes – we see his historicism reduced to revocation, regret, nostalgia and transforming (...) the present into something already concluded, sterile"[25]. Siciliano is not the only one emphasising the fictional over the historical side of Bassani. A sense of moral duty toward a lost world, a personal trauma may have contributed to his fictional evocation. From an analogous perspective, Douglas Radcliff-Umstead, author of a monograph on Bassani entitled *The Exile into Eternity*, sees all the conflicting emotions of the writer as an effort to overcome the shock of rejection[26].

On the other hand, there are some critics who see Bassani's supposed duality as a higher form of expression. The already mentioned Anna Dolfi confirms that in Bassani's narrative the different elements meet in the final message of the writer:

"The historical and biographical events, therefore, blend well and the tragic consciousness of belonging to a different (...) race becomes the existential instrument to express the human and historical destiny of misery, together with a contradictory love of what is 'other' (...)"[27].

Another commentator, Giorgio Varanini, speaks of the deep integration in Bassani of fiction and history. The originality of Bassani's story depends upon his knowledge not only of the existential problems of the people, but also of the specific historical context, where they lived[28].

Bassani himself stresses the importance of the historical events that marked his youth. Although the declarations of a writer are not always the best interpretative key to his work, they can nevertheless cast light on some important questions. In an interview, Bassani declares that his art is founded on realism and on the personal experience of Fascism. Given his 'allergy' to generalisations, he has not written sociological essays on *The* Fascism; he has rather deepened a local event for moral and individual reasons. "I think I am historicist enough to know that Fascism is a precise fact (...) Fascism was useful for research and an explanation of the events of my youth, of my moral experience. Hence, I refer always to a very particular fascism, to its historical reality, both Po-Valley and Ferrarese"[29].

2 Benevolence and Betrayal

Gli ex fascistoni di Ferrara
invecchiano
alcuni
di quelli che nel '39
mostravano di non più ravvisarmi
traversano mi buttano
come a Geo le braccia al collo
gaffeurs incontenibili
sospirano eh voi
propongono
dopo la dolorosa
pacca sulla spalla mancina
l'agape casalinga
che alfine consenta alla monumentale mummy cattolica
d'estrazione bolognese o rovigotta
ai brucanti in tinello strabiondi
teen-agers incontaminati
di incontarlo una buona volta
il già compagno di scuola talmente
bravo
il bravo
romanziere
il presidente...

Hanno l'aria di insinuare
nel mentre dài piantala
non vedi che sei tu quoque
mezzo morto?
E poi scusa – continuano

uguali identici ormai
all'ingegner Marcello
Rimini
al rabbino dottor Viterbo –
in che altro modo senza di
noi
avresti potuto metterle insieme
le tue balle con relativo
appoggio di grana eccetera? Dopo tutto
cazzo
potresti ben cominciare
a considerarci anche noi quasi dei mezzi...

Corrazziali? Voi quoque? Dei quasi
mezzi cugini? No piano
Come cazzo si
fa?

Prima
cari
moriamo

G. Bassani: "Gli ex fascistoni di Ferrara"[30]

1. The Myth of the Good Italian

Alexander Stille has entitled his book on five Italian-Jewish families "Benevolence and Betrayal" to underline the complex situation of the Jews in Italy[31]. The fact is that a long coexistence of Jews and non-Jews had characterised the peninsula; Fascism itself had ruled Italy for sixteen years before anti-Semitic legislation was introduced. The following events, then, cast the Italian Jews in the deepest confusion. A great part of post-war historiography reflects this inner ambivalence. While explaining the history of the Italian Jews and even the Fascist persecution, they unconsciously preserve a myth. Attilio Milano is still one of the main references for the history of the Jews in Italy. Milano's history starts from the first centuries BC and ends in the 1950s. It goes through the institution of ghettos, the religious discriminations and, finally, the Fascist persecutions. However, the essay is based on the assumption that Italy was really the *I-tal-ia*, in Hebrew the Isle of the divine dew. To the historian, who during the Second World War had found refuge in Israel, Italy remains a wonderful country. In fact, for him, "the residence of the Jews in Italy has been, on the whole, one of the happiest experienced by a Jewish group in the Diasporic life"[32]. To the Italians, Milano attributes an affability and tolerance, which permitted a peaceful coexistence lasting about two-thousand years. Compared with other European

8

countries, Italy lacks any political or religious intransigence, while a diffused spontaneity rules. "In having the Italians understood and tolerated and the Jews respected and appreciated, lies the explanation of such an ancient coexistence"[33].

Attilio Milano recalls how the beauty of Italy affected the imagination of the Jews. For them, Italy came to represent the symbol of the Promised Land or the terrestrial embodiment of Paradise. This contributed in creating a true affection for the country and a persistent memory of fortunate periods, such as the Renaissance, which could be at the heart of the myth of the Good Italian. For Stuart Hugues, on the other hand, it was the persistence of the ghetto and the particularities of its condition which left a nostalgic mentality[34]. "Such was the final irony of the Italian ghettos: in rare and privileged instances, those dank abodes might shimmer in the sentimentalising glow of recollection as warm and cozy nooks – and hence as an emotional resource worth preserving long after the threshold of assimilation had been crossed"[35].

In the modern era, the question of Jewish emancipation was not the object of many controversies. The emancipation and the closure of ghettos were brought about for the first time by the Napoleonic army in the late 18th century. It was a brief experience of fourteen years, followed by the harsh period of Restoration. Nevertheless, the democratic ideals of the Revolution continued to inspire the whole *Risorgimento*. Maurizio Molinari has stressed the strict relation between the Italian movement for independence and the Jews. The national claims of the *Risorgimento* not only influenced the Zionist movement, but involved as such the majority of the Italian Jews. They actively participated in the unification of Italy, rightly foreseeing the possibility of achieving once and for all full citizenship. After the creation of Italy, in 1861, many were the Jews elected as deputies, ministers or mayors. In 1889, a new legislation, named 'codice Zanardelli', cancelled any distinction between the State religion and the other faiths. In this liberal atmosphere, however, there were also some exceptions, such as the case of Pasqualigo[36]. Despite these, the process of emancipation seemed successful and the majestic synagogue of Rome, founded in 1904, stood out as its symbol.

Obviously, such radical changes were not without effects on the Jewish communities of Italy. Molinari describes the progressive transformation of the Italian Jews into Jewish Italians. There were three main reactions on the Jewish part: assimilation, integration and ethnical differentiation, that is, Zionism. The majority of Italian Jews chose the first, accepting the national values and making of religion a moral system, rather than a way of life. In this sense, they behaved like most of the Italian people. The same is also valid in relation to Fascism, which was not immediately identified as a violent and racist movement. On the contrary, it appeared at the beginning as the defender of those traditional values that many Jews felt as their own. So, in defence of property, family, co-operation between workers and employers and national pride, 750 Jews registered to the National Fascist Party (PNF) in 1922. They were the so-called 'first-hour' Fascists, whom the Racial Laws would have treated as a privileged category. In 1928, the number of Jewish Fascists increased to 1770, arriving in 1933 to 4800. Yet there were also many Jews, such as the Rosselli brothers, who had immediately reacted to the Fascist regime, grasping its antidemocratic nature. They founded the Resistance groups, known as 'Giustizia e libertà' (Justice and Freedom), and 'Partito d'Azione' (Action Party), inspired by communist ideals. Nevertheless, the majority of Jews, once again like the Italian party, showed a certain naïf indifference to the political system[37].

This is why, in an atmosphere of almost complete assimilation, the Racial Laws of November 1938 caused confusion and astonishment among the Italian Jews. It was a cultural and moral shock, though the Italian population seemed to react to the anti-Semitic campaign with the usual apathy. Renzo De Felice holds that the anti-Semitic propaganda of the period provides an indirect documentation of the resulting dissent. So, the number of articles attacking the so-called 'Pietism' shows, in fact, the strength of resistance to the anti-Semitic legislation[38].

Leon Poliakov remarks on the supposed Italian imperviousness to anti-Semitism, attributing a 'wise nature' to the Mediterranean people. "It seems that the infection of racist propaganda, which more probably attacks barbaric people, finds an ideal ground in the northern climates"[39]. The work of Poliakov and Sabille on the Jews under the Italian occupation stresses the exemplary behaviour of the Italian army in Southern France, Croatia and the Greek Islands. In those dominions, the lowest soldier as well the highest ranking official tried to defend the Jews from the Vichy troops, the Ustashas and the German army. Through a policy of negotiation and bureaucratic obstacles, the Italian army succeeded in saving hundreds of lives or, at least, in delaying as much as possible the capture of the Jews. Poliakov's introductory statement seems to clarify the psychological urge of this otherwise documented historical research. "In recent years our history has been too much one of delusions and bitterness not to appreciate the warm humanity of the Italian people (...) "[40].

Also the more recent book of Susan Zuccotti speaks of the brave and decent response of many Italians in face of the persecution of the Jews. The historian does not omit cases of collaboration, betrayal, opportunism. Nevertheless, she sharply distinguishes the Italian population from the Fascist government. To her, the 'favourable balance' of the Jewish victims in Italy is a positive result of individualism and 'the amiable inclination to ignore the law' of many Italian people and Jews[41].

2. The Counter-myth of the Italian Diffidence

Is Italy really a good country, the isle with divine dew? Are the Jews who disappeared from the peninsula during the last World War a modest number?

The latest researches in this field tend to confirm the opposite. Moreover, they try to demonstrate, against the traditional historiography, how anti-Semitism has been a national product, profoundly bound to Italian culture and policy. One of the leaders of the new historical trend is the historian Liliana Picciotto Fargion, president of the C.E.D.E.C. (Centre for the Jewish Documentation) of Milan and author of *The Book of Memory*. The historian underlines the responsibility of Italian Ministers and Institutions in organising the perse-

cutory policy. The Italian troops of the R.S.I., the Social Republic of Italy, also participated in the raids and arrests. Moreover, five years of anti-Semitic legislation had already
provided the 'initial phase', the bureaucratic one, of the persecution. That is why in Italy
the operations of identification, imprisonment and deportation of the Jews were particularly rapid and efficient. Picciotto Fargion describes attentively the conditions of life in the
Italian concentration camps. She notes: "In the arrangement of the provincial camps at the
beginning, then the camp of Fossoli, as a concentration camp specifically for Jews, one
sees the phase of the complete Italian responsibility".[42] Also she distinguishes between the
behaviour of the population and that of the authorities, and above all, between the royal
Fascist policy and that of the Fascist Republic. Nevertheless, the overlapping of Fascism
with Nazism and the raising of a violent anti-Semitism were the only possible develop-
ments of Fascism. They were inscribed from the beginning in its totalitarian dream of 'the
new man', the 'Fascist man', who was the prototype of the ethnic and spiritual perfection
of the Italian race[43].

With regard to this anti-Semitism, Enzo Collotti emphasises the internal reasons for
it, rather than external pressure from Nazi Germany. The aim of the Fascist regime was to
obtain consensus by marginalising the 'other'. The Jew in this case, as in so many others,
was suitable for representing many dangers: he was at once the Bolshevik and the pluto-
crat, the revolutionary and the hateful oppressor, the marginal figure from the ghetto and
the shadow of International Finance. Collotti denounces the reticence of historians about
the importance of the Racial Laws and persecution of the Jews. This was a strategy of dis-
guising the Italian responsibility, reinforcing the common idea of the faults of Germany[44].

More radical in his criticism is the historian Davide Bidussa, who speaks of the
specificity of Italian anti-Semitism. In his opinion, the Italian Racial Laws have their own
coherence and autonomy from the Nazi legislation. He is very critical toward the major
historians of the Jews in Italy – Cecil Roth, Arnaldo Momigliano, Renzo De Felice – who
have presented a mild image of Italian hostility against the Jews. Bidussa attributes to
Italy a form of 'differential racism', directed not against racial, but cultural differences. It
is what Mussolini had christened the 'spiritual racism' of Italy, against by the 'biologic'
doctrine of Germany[45]. This trend, together with the individualism and the indifference of
many Italian people, is the cultural background of Italian anti-Semitism[46].

In a text specifically devoted to the deconstruction of the myth of the good Italian,
Bidussa demonstrates its falsity. Racism and anti-Semitism do exist in Italy, they have
always been secret currents of hatred. For Bidussa, Italy is a contradictory country, more
Ancient than Modern, and which has reacted to Modernity, with an irrational fear of the
alien. In this respect, the Jew has been the perfect embodiment of the sinister, menacing
foreigner. Besides, Italian anti-Semitism had already been fed with Catholic and national-
istic myths, whose respective aims were to reinforce a religious and a national identity.
"The Racial Laws *describe* and *prescribe* not only who is no more Italian, but, above all,
what *has to be* the Italian citizen"[47].

Clearly for these and for many other historians, who dismantle the notion of a good
or accidental Italian anti-Semitism, some events, whose importance has been ignored,

become crucial. As an example, the Rocco Laws of 1930–1931, legalising Jewish organisations in Italy, are not only a recognition of their legal status, they are also a better way of controlling the Jews and reducing their pluralism. By the same token, the census of Jewish population in 1938 was essential to identify, count and define the designated victims. The racial legislation itself and the hundreds of following decrees are examined no more as incoherent norms, issued by a mild, 'Italian style' dictator[48].

For these authors, the case of Pasqualigo is not an exception, rather a sign of general mistrust. If during the process of emancipation the Jews were really integrated into Italian society, how could they be discriminated against, expelled and persecuted, eighty years later? Is the massive anti-Semitic campaign attributable solely to 'external pressures'? Why the segregation of foreign Jews in 1940? And what about the infamous 'Carta di Verona' of November 1943, where all the Jews were declared foreigners and therefore enemies? This marks actually the beginning of a *legal* persecution. To these questions, Simona Urso gives an answer that denies that true harmony has ever occurred in Italy or elsewhere in the West. To her, acceptance and persecutory process, in fact, "live together in the relationship between Jewish and Western culture. This contradiction (...) is, on the contrary, the cause of a collective repression, of the tendency to forget"[49]. As a proof of it, it would be enough to consult some of the best literature on the destruction of the Jews[50]. Perhaps, the forgetfulness of the role played by Italy depends on the supposed exiguity of the victims; perhaps it is a new version of an old myth[51].

3. Ferrara, a Microcosm of Fascism

If the historian Paul Corner is right, "it was in Ferrara that the potentiality of Fascism emerged clearly"[52]. It was here, in fact, that Fascism, in the early twenties, became a precise movement against the socialists and the day labourers. In this town, the 'Fascist action squads' of Italo Balbo received the support of the agrarian bourgeoisie, giving a significant example to the rest of Italy. Since Jews played an important role in this process, it can be interesting to follow the different stages in the history of Ferrarese Jewry. Moreover, this will become crucial in the context of Bassani's narrative.

The first settling of Jews in Ferrara is very ancient, dating from the 4th century B.C. They were merchants and shopkeepers from Rome. The Estes, the noble family ruling over Ferrara, seemed to understand immediately the advantages of having Jews in their dominions and the Jews first achieved legal permission to settle in Ferrara in 1275.

Attilio Milano, in his *History of the Jews in Italy*, describes the Estense Ferrara as a perfect example of harmony between Italian lords and Jews, despite the pressures of the Church. In 1481, they could legally build the Italian synagogue. Soon after, the various waves of immigrants established a Spanish-rite synagogue, a German, a Portuguese one. The Dukedom of Ferrara became a refuge for the Jews expelled from Spain, Central Europe and other parts of Italy[53]. By the 16th century, the Jews of Ferrara made up more that 2000 of a population of about 10,000. They were a heterogeneous mix of Italian,

German, Spanish and Portuguese Jews. Beside, it was a lively and cultivated community, provided with ten synagogues and a specific university for the study of the Talmud and Hebrew. Hence, Ferrara emerged as the major Italian centre for Talmudic studies[54].

Although in the Estes dominions the main tendency was to protect and respect the Jews, the concessions were compensated with some returns. So, in 1458, the Jews had to pay a high penalty to the Inquisition for having built a synagogue without permission. During the period of the Counter-Reformation, the Estes accepted the burning of the Talmud and later, in 1581, they handed in three Marranos to the Tribunal of the Inquisition. The fact is that the Estes cared more for the economic welfare of their dominion than the well-being of the Jews.

In any case, the situation for the Jews changed dramatically under Church rule. In 1598, the Church occupied Ferrara, taking advantage of a dynastic vacancy. Immediately, the Jews were the object of humiliating restrictions: they had to wear a yellow badge and they could not possess any real estate. From the point of view of the cult, the number of synagogues was limited to three and the sacred texts submitted to dogmatic controls. As a direct consequence, in 1601 the Jewish community of Ferrara had decreased to 1500 people. In 1626, they were enclosed in the ghetto and the exchanges with Christians were harshly forbidden. The only contacts were on Sunday, when a fixed number of Jews crossed the boundaries to attend convertional sermons. In the street, the Jews were so mocked and injured by the local population, that the Jewesses were relieved of the obligation. During the 17th and the 18th centuries, then, the ghetto was attacked several times. Yet, in 1721 a blood libel charge arose.

With the French occupation, the Jews obtained the first emancipation. In 1796, the gates of the Ferrara ghetto were opened and the Jews could fully participate in the social and economic life of the town. Nevertheless, the new era lasted just fourteen years, until the defeat of Napoleon. After it, a reactionary regime was restored, which deprived the Jews of their recent acquisitions. During the period of Restoration, the prohibitions, although weakened by the revolutionary experience, persisted. The oppressions imposed particularly by Pope Pius IX culminated in 1856, with a military raid within the ghetto of Ferrara. The answer of the Jews was to intensify their participation in the Risorgimento, trusting the liberal ideals of the national movement. For example, a few years after the assault on the ghetto, the National Guard of Ferrara included 126 Jews. In 1863, with the annexation of the papal dominions into the Italian constitutional monarchy, the state of confinement of Ferrarese Jewry seemed to cease. Despite the long separation, the Jews of Ferrara succeeded in integrating themselves into the city's professional circles. In a few years, they became the representatives of the urban and agrarian bourgeoisie of Ferrara. It was precisely this role that led many of them to support the rising Fascism. Corner, who has specifically studied the origin of Fascism in Ferrara, underlines the rural and conservative character of this early movement. In contrast to the urban Fascism of Milan, which was mainly political and subversive, that of Ferrara was a violent defence of economic interests and of the *status quo*[55]. Ferrara, moreover, taught the Fascist leadership the best strategy for seizing power, that is, violence and violation of any liberal norm. In May

1922, for example, the troops of Balbo occupied Ferrara, showing how easily they could win the legal powers of the State. This episode created a precedent for the well-known March on Rome. Corner reminds us of the high degree of assimilation of the Ferrarese Jews by that time. In particular, the Jewish landowners, industrialists and traders shared the same conservative tendencies as the Christian party. "Nothing shows that in this period the Jewish community did not behave according to its economic interests"[56].

A different opinion is expressed by Bruno Pincherle, who, although admitting the high percentage of Fascist Jews in Ferrara, holds that their mentality was profoundly anti-Fascist. Theirs was perhaps a liberal anti-Fascism more than a democratic one; they were perhaps more theoretical than active anti-Fascists[57]. The fact was that the Fascism from 1922 to 1938 had not shown any programmatic anti-Semitism and that the process of reciprocal integration had not been interrupted. Before the Racial Laws, for example, Renzo Ravenna, a Jew, was both Mayor of Ferrara and 'first-hour' Fascist. However, a formal link to Fascism was not yet a proof of Fascist faith. Franco Schönheit, a Jew deported from Ferrara, testifies to the general atmosphere of opportunism. "Many Italian people, Jews and Non-Jews, joked that the initials of the party, PNF (Partito Nazionale Fascista) stood for *per necessità familiare* – 'for family necessity' "[58].

Following Pincherle, the discrimination was not passively accepted by Jews. Already before 1938, a handful of anti-Fascist Jews had resisted the many impositions of the dictatorship. Since the June of 1938, 25 Jews had been arrested in Ferrara for anti-Fascist activities. Some of them, like Giorgio Bassani, were put in prison; others were sent to the Italian detention centres or to internment[59].

Whether the Ferrarese Jews supporting Fascism were many or not, unconscious or responsible, they all became the victims of a regime hostile to the Jews.

In autumn 1936, on the wall of Ferrara there appeared some insults against the Jews and the infamous 'Death to the Jews'. In September 1941, the old German-rite synagogue was destroyed by Fascist thugs. At the end of the same year, some Jews were called up for enforced labour[60]. The most tragic phases in the history of the Jews of Ferrara came with the armistice, in September 1943 and the following Nazi occupation.

In November 1943, after the murder of a local Fascist leader, 74 people were arrested, half of whom were Jews. Of the 14 victims shot, four were Jews and three of them, with no record of any political activism.

From the autumn of 1943 to the spring of 1945, about 82 Jews were arrested and deported out of a population of 800 Jews[61]. Their first stop was generally Fossoli, but the final term was rather Auschwitz or Buchenwald for the luckiest. From that journey, only five returned. After the war, the Jewish population of Ferrara was reduced to 200.

3 The Document by Bassani

*Guardami ti prego esclusivo Iddio dei più vecchi dall'amaro
e deliziato sport d'abbandonarmi
– giusto come toccò a mio padre a partire circa dal '30 fino ad almeno
il '38 e le leggi della Razza -*

*nelle braccia del ceto moderato italiano eternamente
traditore e incolpevole da sempre
fascista e innocente*

*scampami te ne supplico – tu che puoi ! – dalle sue dolci
femmine dalle promesse dei loro intatti quasi infiniti
cari gerghi cattolico-agricoli da tutto quanto
so che di esse
forse più amo e più abomino al mondo più adoro ed
esecro*

G. Bassani: "15 giugno 1975 [62]

1. Reading through History

1.1 A Documented Case

Reading the *Romanzo* is not a simple task. At first, we trust the title, seeing the whole book as a novel; then, considering the fragmentation of the various stories, novels and tales, we think rather of a collection of independent works. On the other hand, the references to the same characters and places recall the narrative plot of the saga. That of Bassani, in any case, is a particular saga because the story of Ferrara's population never prevails over the individuality of the characters. There is nothing like a collective mind; it is only by observing the separate characters that, at the end of the *Romanzo*, one can perhaps grasp an 'overall picture'. This in its turn acquires coherence only thanks to the historical framework. Without knowledge of Ferrarese Fascism, the weight and the consequences of the discrimination of 1938, Bassani's heroes would seem affected by a pathological persecution complex. They always react; the point is to discover the reasons for and the object of their subversive tendency.

As an example of Bassani's writing, we could examine briefly the stories regarding Bruno Lattes. This character appears several times in the *Romanzo*, the first time is in *The Last Years of Clelia Trotti*. Here he is described in the autumn of 1946, returned from America for the funeral of his old teacher. Being in Ferrara again reminds him of the time seven years before, when he had reacted against discrimination with a new faith in class struggle. Now Bruno seems definitely disillusioned and detached from everything. The only sign of the old feelings appears when he fixes on a couple of young, blond lovers. They seem to him so pure, so precious, unreachable. Something more of his life is revealed in *The Garden of the Finzi-Continis*. Bruno was one of the young people, who went every afternoon to the garden to play tennis. His tennis partner and lover was Adriana Trentini, a charming girl with long legs and vampish features. Some gossips, following the disappearance of Bruno from circulation, inform the reader that Adriana has left him. It is the time of the anti-Semitic campaign and her lover has already been excluded from the tennis club and thus from the possibility of becoming the local champion. Her behaviour has nothing surprising about it, since she figures from the beginning as a selfish and hypocritical person. *More News of Bruno Lattes*, finally, is the last story centred on this character. It focuses on the moment of the actual break between Bruno and Adriana. This had occurred a few months before the introduction of the Racial Laws, apparently without reason; Adriana had found a justification for a sudden desire for freedom: she was too young, just seventeen years old... One year after, Bruno is still obsessed by the big, rosy, naked body of Adriana. In a moment of despair, he finds her in Abbazia, where he discovers the true cause of their estrangement. In the Grand Hotel, which is the setting for their last meeting, he finds only the indifference and the dull Fascism of the family.

This example demonstrates that the narrative of Bassani does not follow the principles of temporal succession or logical causality. It does, in fact, quite the opposite and only at the end can we fully comprehend the strange attraction that the blond couples exerted on Bruno at the beginning. Bassani tends to hint at indirect clues as the only possible interpretative key. However, the historical facts always stand as the main reference for understanding Bruno's personality. The story of Bruno, finally, mirrors the bitter disillusion of the Jews who have experienced an assimilation that did not seem problematic till it was harshly denied[63].

The case of Bruno, in summary, helps to illustrate the complexity and the diversity of the *Romanzo*. The stories concerning Bruno are not simply fictional stories; they rather show at once the historical context of Fascist Ferrara, the literary strategy of the writer and the soul of an assimilated Italian Jew. In this way, the whole *Romanzo* becomes a document at once of historical, narrative and personal questions. The three aspects – the historical, the literary and the autobiographical – are strictly interwoven in the *Romanzo*, in accordance with Bassani's persona, who is at once historical witness, writer and assimilated Jew of Ferrara.

1.2   A Jewish Picture of Ferrara

From the point of view of history, the *Romanzo* documents the condition of life of the Ferrarese Jewish community in many ways. Bassani describes what Ada Neiger has called 'the Jewish civilisation' or the ethnicity[64]. The synagogues, the Jewish cemetery, the decorations and the main festivals are all present in a detailed picture.

The majority of the descriptions are contained in 'The Garden' and their subjects are religious. Through this novel, we acknowledge not only the difference between the synagogues of diverse rite, but also the importance of following a particular rite. According to Bassani, the German-rite synagogue was the harshest; the Levantine, that is, the French one, was just for a few families; the little Spanish-rite had fallen into disuse; while the Italian synagogue had assumed the popularity and theatricality of the Catholic Church. Inside the Italian-rite synagogue, which Bassani calls occasionally Temple or more frequently School, the women went up into the gallery, provided with gratings, which allowed them to attend the service. The men sat in pews, holding the old familiar talèd. To one side, passed the procession of the sefarìm, wrapped in short silk mantels and displaying the Torah scrolls. The service ended with the gathering of all the children under the taledòt of their family and the recitation of the final benediction, the berehà. The ones who knew Hebrew repeated the words of the prayer together with the rabbi, the others kept silence, not without a certain embarrassment. Bassani refers to the synagogue not only as a place of worship, but also as a meeting place where people socialise.

In the first of the two tales at the end of the *Romanzo*, Miss Egle Levi-Minzi, the eternal spinster, "neither ugly, nor poor, nor stupid, nor mature"[65], falls in love with the Ukrainian Yuri Rotsein right in the synagogue. "He looked upstairs, toward the side of the women's gallery, with his wonderful, smiling, winking, wild blue eyes (...) It was clear that the young man had not greeted her, but the old farmer sat at her side, his mother. And nevertheless, she pretended to have misunderstood (...) ?"[66].

The Jewish cemetery is even more present than the synagogue in Bassani's stories. In all of them, it is at least mentioned in passing, as a topographical point of reference. Moreover, on many occasions, it becomes the main arena of confrontation for the 'secular' Jews and the Jewish traditions. Sometimes it creates a rupture between Catholics and Jews. When the son of Elias Corcos died, the burying of his body in the Jewish cemetery constituted the first explicit mark of difference between his Judaism and the Catholicism of his wife. In attending to what she perceived as a strange rite, the woman threw herself on the dead child, claiming that "she did not want to leave her poor baby there"[67]. Before that death, Elias Corcos has not bothered so much about his Judaism. He had chosen, on the contrary, to live outside the Jewish quarter of Ferrara and even to stop paying his annual contribution to the Jewish community. Nevertheless, when his son dies, he does not want him to be cut off from the collective memory.

The Finzi-Continis have the same cult of the dead, building for their family a monumental tombstone in the Jewish cemetery of Ferrara. This is the reason why their history is evoked by a visit to the Etruscan necropolis at Cerveteri. Nevertheless, places of death are more than a monument for nostalgic commemoration. They are symbols of the continuity of life, of the past's vitality.

With regard to house decoration, there are in Bassani references to the mezuzòt. They appear in all the Jewish houses as beloved and respected objects, while provoking in the non-Jews a special curiosity and some trouble.

Bassani also quotes occasionally the 'giudeo-ferrarese', the Jewish-Ferrarese dialect of the old Ferrarese Jews. It is particularly in *The Walk before Dinner* that it is reported as the 'mysterious language', the 'ghetto jargon' of the Jews. The one using it is mainly old Salomon Corcos, Elia's father, who lived within the ghetto walls. The Jewish-Ferrarese dialect sounds similar to the local dialect, but it remains incomprehensible for the 'guyà', the Gentile daughter-in law of Salomon. Vocabulary such as hamòr (donkey), hasír (pig), magnòd (money), mahòd (beats), pèhat (fear) indicate in some way what was the subject of the conversations[68].

1.3 The Stages of Assimilation

If Bassani records the ethnic aspect of the Jewish community of Ferrara, he does not forget the crucial moments of its history. He always mentions the Estes Castle as the symbol of Ferrara. This is also an indirect commemoration of the 'golden age' of the Renaissance, the mythic period when Jews benefited from an era of tolerance and cultural flourishing. Marilyn Schneider, dealing with the symbolism of Ferrara's map in Bassani, says that the Estes Castle is not only the true heart of the city, but also the symbol of good government. This point of view, continues the critic, casts a new light on the Fascist massacre that occurred against its walls. "The Estes Castle (...) rises at the spatial centre of the city and symbolises the collective unity. The bloodying of this monument (...) is an act of violence that implicitly mocks the traditional foundation rite of the *polis*"[69].

The period of the Risorgimento and the liberation from the ghetto are told with emotional participation from the already mentioned Salomon, who has also been a participant in those events. In those days, Salomon shared the same political tastes as many Italian people. He could not stand the Austrian soldiers, guarding the Archbishop's Palace, while he devoted all his admiration to 'the hero of the two worlds', Giuseppe Garibaldi. Above all, Salomon never forgot that wonderful night in 1861, "when the ghetto gates were pulled down by public acclaim"[70].

The ensuing events of the emancipation and assimilation are directly visible in the social and economical position of Bassani's Jewish characters. They all come from an upper-bourgeoisie, who had bought its lands and real properties immediately after the Italian emancipation. In traditionally rural Ferrara, there were very few industrialists and Bassani rather depicts Jewish landowners, like the Finzi-Continis, and Jewish professionals, lawyers like the fathers of Giorgio and Bruno, or doctors, like Elias. Many of the latter, however, do not practise their profession, being supported by the income from their investments. The social resentment of the position of the Jews, no more newcomers than the Italian bourgeoisie, is expressed quite rarely. The Ferrarese population seems either used to the social hierarchy or openly revolutionary. In both cases, there is no distinction between a Jew and a non-Jewish master. The servants of the Finzi-Continis, for example, are as friendly and faithful as those of Edgardo Limentani. They are respectful figures, ready to obey and protect their lords, similar to the last feudal vassals. Also the left-wingers do not show any particular diffidence to the Jews as such, except as representatives of the privileged class. The peasants who have no direct contact with the Jews show more frankly than the others the ambivalence of their feelings. It is a mix of ignorance and curiosity, a sense of separateness and of indifferentism. As a proof of it, the rural parents of Emma Brondi accept her strange marriage to Elias, but this does not stop them from feeling the distance. The couple's house reflects their inner division, presenting an elegant, urban front and a rustic back, similar to a farm. The parents of the groom enter by the main entrance; while Emma receives her humble familiars at the back. Once again, one can attribute the separation to a question of class, more than to the race of Elias. The first time he introduces himself to the Brondis, they immediately perceive that the man does not belong to their rural environment, but to an aristocratic one. "In relation to this, any other consideration, including that he was not Catholic but Jewish, or better 'Israelite' as he himself specified, was going to become secondary"[71].

1.4 The Anti-Semitism 'Behind the Door'

The text where the anti-Semitic prejudice really appears, well before the Racial Laws, is *Behind the Door*. It is Luigi Pulga, the skinny and vaguely repulsive class-mate from Bologna, who embodies the true, the inner enemy. At the beginning, in fact, Pulga plays the role of the stranger in need, the friend to be protected or, alternatively, the stooge. In this manner, he has access to the house and to the intimacy of Giorgio. His final betrayal, in any case, dismantles a profound hostility against Giorgio, his family and the 'Jewish habits'. The circumcision is defined immodestly as 'taking off the hood'[72]; the kindness of Giorgio's mother, a wild sensuality, hinting of nymphomania[73]. "She was a woman about thirty-three, thirty-five years old – continued [Luciano] – maybe a little 'flabby' as Jewesses always are, but with what a mouth, what big brown eyes and, especially, what an intense look"[74]. At the same time, the emotional and economic stability of Giorgio's father transforms into the obtuseness of the cuckolded. The mezuzòt are described as silly, strange circles, like coins, written in 'Hebrew' and Giorgio's Judaism, on the other hand, is nothing but an incredible pride, making God a familiar grandpa. In short, the insults that Giorgio listened to behind the door, must have been the first real betrayal of his life, a hint of those to follow, a summary of all of them. The author, in fact, opens the novel with this confession:

> "Many times I have been unhappy in my life (...) many times, if I think on it, I have touched the alleged bottom of despair. Yet I remember few periods so dark for me as the school-months (...) when I attended the first class at high-school. (...) a pain (...) has remained there like a secret wound, secretly bleeding"[75].

That of Pulga is a perfect manifesto, a sinister mainstream of vulgar anti-Semitism. It is based on a wider social and sexual resentment, which exploits morbid curiosities. As such, it involves also the usual mechanism of projection, which attributes to the Jews the worst personal faults of the anti-Semites. In speaking of the supposed instability of Giorgio, Pulga explains it as an attribute of his Jewishness. "He knew from experience what characteristic instability must be expected from a Jew"[76]. In these respects, this violent anti-Semitism is the opposite of the calm and aristocratic, almost completely hidden, anti-Semitism of Cattolica. Carlo Cattolica is the other, the positive pole of Pulga: he is the best student in the class; despite sharing a desk with Giorgio, he does not need him for he has already got his clique of subjugated friends. Moreover, as the surname itself indicates, he comes from a very Catholic family, one of the most distinguished of Ferrara. Cattolica never acts like an anti-Semite; on the contrary, he plays the role of the defender of Giorgio. He warns him of the evil nature of Pulga; he organises that painful meeting, which has marked Bassani's life. Despite appearances, Cattolica is not much better than Pulga. The only difference is that he is an insider instead of a foreigner; rich, attractive and cultivated, instead of being a 'parasite'. The only moment when Cattolica lets the mask slip – what irony! – is right inside the Church of Jesus[77]. Giorgio and Carlo meet, under the shadow of the sacred statues, and this is the occasion for Cattolica to pose a lot of questions on Judaism to his class-mate. The latter answers with great emotion and, at the peak of his enthusiasm, asks in his turn whether or not Cattolica may be a Jewish surname. The other reacts as if his good Catholic breeding had been insulted. "He became rigid. 'Here, you are wrong' – he abruptly replied, while assuming a sudden attitude of expertise. 'It is true that many Israelites have surnames of cities and countries. But not all of them (...) I could quote to you an infinite number of cases of people with surnames that seem Hebrew, instead, they are not at all so' "[78].

1.5 Refusal and Rejection

Bassani does not recall the trauma of betrayal and discrimination as merely personal experiences, bound to the individuals' reactions. He also presents them as epochal events, involving the social and political situation of the whole of Ferrara. The Racial Laws enable the potential anti-Semites to reveal publicly their animosity, without any caution. Already during the anti-Semitic campaign, Mrs Lavezzoli, a fervent Fascist sympathising with the Germans, can no longer refrain from saying that the Jews have in some way deserved their persecution. This is perhaps a sign of divine punishment. As a consequence, the young protagonist of *The Gold-rimmed Eyeglasses*, evades any social contact and chooses for himself a deliberate isolation. He no longer feels at ease in the central street of Ferrara. From the reaction of the local people, he believes he is recognised as somehow different from what he has always known himself to be. An unbridgeable gap seems to be open between the Jews and the 'Goyìm' of Ferrara. It is in this same novel that young Bassani, exasperated by the lack of sensibility of a Christian friend, resurrects the hostile term. "And while Nino, embarrassed, kept silent, I felt arising inside me with incredible disgust the ancient, ancestral hatred of the Jews against anything that is

Christian, Catholic, in sum, *Goi*"[79].

Bassani tells also of the consequences of the 'physical persecution' of the Jews, enacted after September 1943. The whole family of the Finzi-Continis disappears; the eighty year-old Elias Corcos and Bruno's parents share the same fate of deportation to Germany. Some of them do not even perceive the danger, living so aloof from the city. Others refuse to accept that the same Fascism they have known and sustained would pay them back with death. The political arguments between the young Jews and their aged fathers demonstrate well that persistent illusion. Italy is more civilised than Germany, those things will never happen here, politics in Italy are not a serious matter and also the Racial Laws are a little concession to the allies. For the rest, it is just appearance, tricks and cleverness. "But you have to admit it: Hitler is bloody insane, whereas Mussolini is what he is, Machiavellian and a turn-coat, as you like, but..."[80] repeats the father to the rebel son who reads Trotsky and foresees the worst.

Geo Josz is the only Ferrarese Jew to survive the death camp. He comes back to Ferrara in the summer of 1945, just in time to correct the plaque recording the 187 Jewish victims of that town. After the war, Ferrara is the same niche of egoism and hypocrisy that had shut the doors in the face of the persecuted. This is the diagnosis of the mature Bruno and the final revelation for Geo. The situation is exactly the same as it was during the massacre in Via Mazzini, when the Ferrarese waited for the Fascists to take their scapegoats[81]. People always fear only for themselves, they are ready to accept compromises to safeguard their tranquillity. They always avoid examining their consciences. The atmosphere of renewal does not convince the rescued. Not only Geo, but also Bruno, Edgardo, Bassani himself could not bear any more to live in the same city that "from 1915 to 1939 (...) had assisted, in Ferrara as everywhere in Italy, in the progressive degeneration of any value"[82].

2. A Literary Strategy

2.1 The Antifascist Style

I have demonstrated the particular narrative strategy of Bassani. It corresponds to an indirect style of writing, whose aim is to evoke the whole environment by dint of single clues. As we have seen, Bassani does not lack a focused attention on his heroes, or better, anti-heroes. Nevertheless, his technique is to describe everything about them and around them, following a circular scheme, that is, from the outside to the inside. Many have stressed the circularity of Bassani's writing. A literary critic has even seen the circle as the structural metaphor of all Bassani's works. His accounts, then, are nothing but a series of circles, inscribed one within another. The first wider circle is that of the memory: the remembrance allows us to pass to the second circle of Ferrara; this in turn contains the third circle of the ghetto; the Finzi-Continis' villa, fourth and the last circle, is the ideal centre of the ghetto[83]. Hence, Bassani's narrative technique drives from the periphery to the centre, thanks to description each time more detailed and focused. The origin of this movement is the individual, whose intimate nature, nevertheless, remains unknown. It is like a pebble thrown into a still pool: the concentric waves reveal only the presence, not the colour and shape of the object.

In an interview with Anna Dolfi, Bassani has confessed: "(...) I do not have the faith of my predecessors (Proust, James) that the deep self can be grasped, known: I do not believe it, I do not believe it any more (...) The self is no more important than what surrounds it"[84]. Elsewhere, Bassani denied any analogy between the nineteenth century romance and his own. What really differentiates his *Romanzo* is the psychological account of the characters, who are not adapted to fit a simplistic scheme. His men and women have, on the contrary, their independence and freedom. Within the one limit of the historical frame, they can decide for themselves. That is why the personalities of the *Romanzo* seem sometimes mysterious, unbearably so. "But he, David, who was he? (...) What was he looking for ?"[85], Lidia wonders recalling their relationship. Similarly, the reasons why Elias marries Emma are unknown. And what about the bizarre behaviour of Geo? His story ends in defining him as an enigma. In reality, many of these alleged mysteries could be easily interpreted. David's affair with Lidia is perhaps the first rebellion against parental control; Elias, in marrying the humble non-Jew, expresses the option of living apart from the Jewish community and from the local bourgeoisie. With regard to Geo, then, his strangeness is perhaps too easily understood. After meeting the Fascist spy of Ferrara, he can no longer forget that the murderers are still alive, while his family have all been swallowed by the crematoria.

The indirect style of Bassani expresses, on the one hand, the guilty conscience of the people pretending not to know; on the other hand, an anti-Fascist position. The mystery of Bassani's characters is a proof of their diversity and independence from cultural levelling. As Renato Bertacchini reminds us, Bassani's prose is profoundly anti-Fascist in showing a continual solidarity with the 'different'. In this respect, the practice of writing fights against the systematic oppression of the exception, typical of any conservatism. This anti-Fascism means both respect for the individual and acceptance of commitment. So, if Bassani rejects the documentaries of Neo-Realism, he does not ignore the dialectic relation between characters and events. Bassani, therefore, expresses the latter using the so-called 'indirect, social talk', which is at once his literary style and his ideological structure. Through this means, Bassani reports the different faiths, fears and hopes of the people without generalising them, rather attributing to anybody his/her own voice[86].

In contrast with the declamatory rhetoric of Fascism and with the straightforward style of Neo-Realism, Bassani makes frequent use of symbolism. It is, in some way, a simple symbolism which does not conceal meanings in complicated metaphors. The language of Bassani, in fact, is clear, simple; it make occasional use of local dialect as well as slang expressions. Bassani's characters, when passing from monologue to dialogue, speak to be understood. If communication fails it is not due to the complexity of their language or thoughts; it is rather the dialogical relation that fails, as I have said above, because of the guilty conscience of the interlocutor. There are few cases where the language is intentionally used as a barrier, as a sign of distinction, isolation or uniqueness. In these moments, the characters turn to a secret language. As an example, Alberto and Micòl

Finzi-Contini have invented a special language full of nuances and secret. It is still Italian, comprehensible to anyone, yet it is mainly the 'finzi-continico', which stresses the complicity of brother and sister. The verses that Elias sometimes recites to his wife have an opposite function. In this case, the Latin or aulic language just increases the cultural gap between them.

Bassani, hence, does not entrust his symbolism to the context of dialogues, in the open words of communication. It is rather present in the internal voice of the characters, in their unspoken reflections and descriptions of the environment. From the point of view of symbolism and signification, the role of mundane object, for example, some parts of the rural and urban landscape, are particularly relevant. So much so that it may be said that they are the actual speakers of the secret language of Bassani. Their subjects are difference, exclusion, split, conflict, in short, the failure of any harmony.

2.2 The Symbols of Distance

One of the most common images in Bassani's *Romanzo* is that of the walls: the walls of the Estes castle, the walls surrounding the city, the walls of the Jewish cemetery, those of the Finzi-Continis' estate and those of the ghetto. They represent the perennial state of exile of the individuals from life and from the others. The wall, in fact, symbolically separates the Jew from the non-Jewish population, the political and cultural centre of Ferrara, the Estes Castle, from the rest of the town and, finally, the whole of Ferrara from the rest of the world. The walls, evoking separateness, silence and the presence of the past, become the metaphor for Jewish and human misery. "Being within the walls is both a duty a condemnation, the at once disputed and denied condition of unhappiness as an acceptance of one's own historical being *hic et nunc*"[87], writes Anna Dolfi. To her, the walls are a series of concentric, parallel cages, each time smaller and more constricting. However, the walls are also a border with an external and internal face. Hence, the dynamic tension of all Bassani's stories, which aim towards an impossible exit or an equally impossible entry. The characters within the walls are prisoners who desire the freedom or, on the contrary, outsiders who try to penetrate the barrier. In the opinion of the critic, in Bassani's stories there is a centrifugal dynamic, whereas in the 'novels of the self', the main force is centripetal[88]. The only exception to this would be *The Heron*, where Edgardo escapes compromise by means of suicide. So his tragic end confirms the unbearable situation of 'being a part of' something. In the words of Radcliff-Umstead, "The ironic situation of salvation through suicide marks the achievement of a creative quest to overcome the destructive fragmentation of human experience"[89].

The role of boundary is also played by all the transparent sheets which substitute for direct sight. I am referring to the eyeglasses, to the window, the mirrors. The eyeglasses of Fadigati, like those of Elias are not only the mark of their being different, apart and reflective in any sense. In the slow and boring afternoons spent in her slum, Lidia looks through the window in search of another reality. The Po-landscape also shrugs off its familiarity if seen from the perspective of train and car windows. The piece of reality framed by the window evokes a picture never seen before. The same impression of extraneity is given by the mirrors as characters catch sight of their own faces with astonishment. "In the oval of the mirror over the washbasin, I saw my face reflected, I observed it carefully as if it belonged to another person"[90]. In this case, the young man is trying to figure out how another person, perhaps the beloved Micòl, can interpret his physiognomy. For the suicidal Limentani, on the contrary, the mirror witnesses a progressive decrease of the vital instincts. In any of these examples, the screen does not simply offer an objective image of reality. It reflects, rather, the outside in the inside of the individual, it transforms the sight into a personal vision and, above all, a vision of the self.

2.3 The Symbol of Deception

The barriers and the boundaries work as obstacles and mediations between the self and the world, the outside as a general term including people, landscapes, urban areas and events. Through them, Bassani always expresses a polarity, but in the case of sexuality the tension is higher. Besides, since sexual relations involve directly and exclusively human beings, they better represent social dynamics. As Marilyn Schneider underlines, Bassani identifies sexuality with sociability to such an extent that any divergence from the "norm" means the failure of the social approach and the condemnation to a sterile existence. In the universe of Bassani, homosexuality, homoeroticism and failed heterosexuality are, in fact, the 'stigmata of difference'[91]. When traces of them appear in the characters, they suggest not simply a personal sexual inclination, but rather a destiny of isolation, illness and perhaps tragic death. Fadigati commits suicide; Alberto Finzi-Contini falls ill and dies; Giorgio himself, at the height of his intimacy with Pulga, has a disease of the throat. Obsession and disgust for sexual relations with women recur also in Limentani, as signs of his imminent death.

In this frame, the sexual state becomes at once the symbol of the social condition, and the mark of physical and mental health[92]. Hence, the difficult relation of Jewish men and Christian women. They stand for the anti-social tendency in many ways: some of them are unmarried, others break the anti-Semitic legislation. Even the few legalised are 'physically' isolated: they live distant from the town and experience, then, a deeper distance from each other. So, as a result of all the difficulties, their unions appear really 'insane', lacking any sexual and psychological agreement. Incidentally, the stereotypical characterisation of women by Bassani tends to divide the female realm into two basic types. On the one side, there are the non-seductive women, such as Jewish mothers or girls; on the other side, there are the seductive, who are Christian women, prostitutes or unfaithful wives. It is true that in this reversal of the myth of the beautiful Jewess, one could see, like Ada Neiger suggests, the projection of the author's frustrations[93]. Nevertheless, I would rather agree with Marilyn Schneider, who sees in it a representation of the political roles. For her, in fact, sexuality is related also to politics, which is one of the main aspects of the social relations. In this sense, the *Romanzo* would show many pairs of opposites, whose sexual and political inclinations are strictly linked. For example, the Fascist Sciagura and the coward Pino Barillari are respectively the dominant-sadistic and the submitted-masochistic[94]. In the light of this interpretation, the sexual aggression is at the same time a political act of violence; the sexual tricks of the 'Aryans' stand for the personal and collective betrayal of the Jews. The sexual passivity of Jews is a representation of their astonishment and impotence in the face of deception and death.

3. The Shaping of Memory

3.1 A Conscience in Progress

Both the historical and the literary analysis of the *Romanzo* have stressed the role of memory. Memory not only permits us to recall the historical situation of the Jews in Ferrara, but also presents the fictional account as results of remembering. The stories of Bassani always appear as personal memories, either belonging directly to the author or to someone else. Even if they start in the present, a simple postcard, a street, a name provide an opportunity to make a backward journey. In recalling the past, Bassani's narrative has just some exterior analogies with that of Proust. As Claudio Varese has rightly noted, the time of Proust is refound because it is irremediably passed, whereas in Bassani the time, even if past, is always present. Sometimes it is interrupted, almost denied and stalled. For the rest, time is an historical and political reality which also enters into the feelings of the characters[95]. Besides, in Bassani's own words, Proust is passive and aesthetic; he himself is active, that is, selective in recalling the past, and moral[96]. Bassani's conception of the past is much more similar to that of Italo Svevo. The writer from Trieste denied the existence of the future, holding that one can write only of what exists, of life as experienced at the time of writing. Similarly, Bassani says: "My poetry, therefore, as well as my narrative, speaks of the past, of the present, and not of the future, because the future is not"[97].

Memory is necessarily linked to that work in progress of forty-years, from 1938 to 1978, whose result is the final version of the *Romanzo*. The continual revising of Bassani's writings is not, as someone said, the tendency to stylistic perfection typical of the poet. Neither is Bassani's explanation of the slow and painful process of writing totally convincing. "It is sure that from the beginning I have always had the greatest difficulty (...) just in writing. No, unfortunately, I have never possessed the famous 'gift'. Also now, while I am writing, I stumble over every word, I risk losing my bearing in the middle of every sentence. I write, I erase, I write again, I erase again. Endlessly"[98].

There must be another, deeper reason for these changes especially as, in the late versions, not only has the language been slightly altered, but also some more important details. As an example, the first version of *More News on Bruno Lattes* was entitled *The Circle of Walls*. The plot of the stories is the same: both open in the Jewish cemetery, during the funeral of the protagonist's uncle. In both, the young man contrasts the negative elements of the Jewish character and the strengths of the Catholics. The differences are that in the oldest version the protagonist, named not Bruno but Gerolamo Camaioli, complains of being similar to his Jewish family, an 'unavoidable condemnation'. In the late version, instead, Bruno expresses his relief at being different from them. "Well, also from the point of view of character, no similarity between him and *them*, thank God, not the slightest"[99]. Perhaps more important is the altered description of the social environment of Ferrara. In the first version, the pensioners sit outside to observe everything, they see the Jewish funerals and react positively. "Although the funeral carts were never surmounted by a cross, they greeted them all the same by making the sign of the cross (...)"[100]. In the last version, instead of this account, there are the farmers transporting their charges of hay along the tiny Via delle Vigne. "So, a funeral happened by just then, coming from the opposite side, alas: it was necessary for the funeral to wait on the way down (...) five, ten minutes, and sometimes even a quarter of hour"[101].

Hence, Bassani expresses a new social and moral consciousness, in a writing that evolves into a historical definition. It is not simply what Radcliff-Umstead defines "a semantic conquest of the past"[102]. Bassani feels compelled to understand the world he has evoked and that he considers neither definitively dead nor resolved into the fiction. This is the personal and moral urge of Bassani in writing the *Romanzo*.

With regard to the first aspect, the personal one, Bassani has presented on several occasions the strict relation between the self of the writer and the character. To Anna Dolfi, Bassani declares: "It is not possible to think of a book like the *Romanzo* of Ferrara without seeing it as history of the self: the most important character in my work is the self, man and artist"[103]. Hence, the years of revision not only of his text, but mainly of his personal and political experiences. Hence, the figures of adolescents so recurrent in his stories, who are contemporaries of the Bassani of that period, perhaps his personification[104]. Besides, Marylin Schneider has underlined the 'act of self-inscription' of Bassani in his *Romanzo*. The patterns of his life and those of his artistic work are so correspondent, that we may read in the *Romanzo* the progressive emergence not only of the world of Bassani, but also his poetic birth, that is, the consciousness of being a writer. So, the progression from the impersonal stories to the 'novels of the self', where the author openly assumes the role of the narrator. This would mark a new awareness about his own position. Bassani reminds us of the moment when the necessity of qualifying himself emerged. It was not enough, he explains, to be a poet, a writing hand. He had written all the Ferrarese stories, without emerging as a subject. This may have been a form of self-defence from the excess of emotional participation. The rhetoric and syntactical schemes had compensated for a heart too fraternal and agreeable. "At that point, Ferrara, the little segregated universe invented by me, would have revealed to me nothing really new (...) then, in the stage of my parochial little theatre, it was clear to me that I had to find an adequate, not secondary position (...)"[105].

3.2 Hinting at the Absent
Despite the indubitable autobiographical vein of the *Romanzo*, Bassani is never the protagonist of his stories. He is rather the reporter, the witness who depicts with an increasing degree of awareness the scene of a personal and collective trauma.

All his stories are either anticipation or immediate consequences of the Shoà. Following Renato Bertacchini, Bassani does not want to be simply a poet for an abstract humanity. "Bassani wants to be the narrator, the witness-poet of those injured, of those victimised heroes, of those subversives and opponents"[106]. Also other authors who have underlined the centrality of the Jewish subject in Bassani's narrative draw the same conclusion. Asked these questions, Bassani himself answers: "I consider, as one of the aims of my art (...) that of avoiding such a damage [the oblivion], of keeping the memory, the recollection. (...) I could not accept a humanity forgetting Buchenwald, Auschwitz, Mathausen. I write to remember that"[107].

Nevertheless, in the *Romanzo* are depicted the beginning and the end of that story, while its centre is significantly missing. What happened from September 1943, when the Finzi-Continis and Elias are deported, to the August 1945, the date of Geo's return?

Bassani has been so precise in recalling the crucial moments of the Ferrarese Jews, from the French occupation to the unification of Italy, from the emancipation to the Racial Laws. The silence on the *actual* death of the Jews is not an omission, but the opposite: the denunciation of the experience of the contemporary Jews, that is, the complete silence of the lager. This is in its turn the silence in and *on* the lager. Once again, Bassani's narration mirrors the emptiness of the collective social mind.

Many texts on the Holocaust literature mention only *The Garden of the Finzi-Continis* as a novel specifically on the destruction of the Jews[108]. I think that the whole *Romanzo*, and not just 'The Garden', evokes that experience. Bassani never writes directly on the Shoà, nor does he ever describe life in a death-camp. This could be interpreted as a strange form of omission or reticence, whereas it is part of his realism. First of all, Bassani describes what he saw. As an Italian Jew living in Ferrara under Fascism, he witnessed the exclusion, the legislative persecution and the deportation of the Jews. Moreover, Bassani possesses a more powerful means of expression for recounting the destruction of the Jews. He inscribes it in the walls of Ferrara, in the local violence and in the subsequent commemorations. In particular, the internal division between Ferrarese Jews and non-Jews becomes progressively an external, irredeemable divorce. A critic has held that the concentration camps are the key to penetrating into Bassani's universe, dominated by death and marginalisation[109]. Death is a dominant presence in the *Romanzo*. It is in the cemeteries, in the cult of the past, in the photographs of the dead, in the collection of decadent objects. In any of Bassani's writings there is at least one death, and the death does not appear, as it traditionally does, at the end of the story. It is very often at the beginning, even in the first lines. *A Plaque in Via Mazzini* opens with the commemoration of the 187 Jews dead in Germany. *The Last Years of Clelia Trotti* places the reader in the civic cemetery of Ferrara. In *A Night in 1943*, an imaginary tourist brushes against the place of the past massacre. From the start of *The Golden -rimmed Eyeglasses*, Fadigati is remembered as a poor man, tragically dead. Finally, for Bassani, death is, above all, violent death from shooting, imprisonment, drowning, suicide or gas. It is the suppression of the different: the impotent, the political enemy, the homosexual, and mostly the Jew. Few characters in Bassani have the privilege of a natural death. All the others, the majority, die for unnatural, that is, social and political reason. *The Garden of the Finzi-Continis*, then, contains the highest number of symbolic references to death, due to the Nazi extermination. The cult of the dead of the Finzi-Continis, their resignation to the present and attachment to the past seem the funereal announcers of their destiny. The chastity of Alberto and Micòl is in itself a refusal of life. Then, the ashes, the walls, the gates, the wind, all refer to imprisonment and the violent death of the family[110]. Some words sound prophetic even when they deal with innocent subject such as love. One night, Giorgio's father reveals to his dear son: "In life, to understand, really understand how worldly things go, one *has* to die at least once. Therefore, since this is the rule, it is better to die when young (...)"[111]. The reasoning on love, hence, the remedy to cure delusions, due to Micòl, are also valid in relation to her premature end.

3.3 A Document of Ambiguity

The *Romanzo* may be read entirely as a commemoration of the Jews murdered by Nazi-Fascists. Yet, the Shoà is not the central issue of the book, for it is represented as the tragic consequence of a process started well before. The marginalisation of the Jews, culminating in the Racial Laws, is the crucial moment of the *Romanzo*. It created a real rupture between Jews and non-Jews, the seriousness of which was directly proportional with the level of assimilation. Since, in Italy, the majority of the Jews had enthusiastically embraced Italian culture, the delusion was great. Psychologically, the betrayal became the symbol of all the previous persecutions and the denial of any supposed integration. It is sufficient to recall what the young Jew of *The Golden-Rimmed Eye-Glasses* repeats to himself, conscious still of the reality. "The future of persecution and massacres that perhaps was in front of us (I have constantly heard of it, since I was a child, as an eventuality always possible for Jews like us) did not frighten me any more"[112]. Another good example comes from 'The Garden' and shows how violent were, after the Racial Laws, the reactions of the new generation against the dream of assimilation. "(...) one of the most hateful forms of anti-Semitism was just this: complaining that the Jews were not enough like the others and then admitting their almost total assimilation in the surrounding environment, complaining of the opposite: that they were just like the others, that is, no different from the average"[113].

It is precisely this moment of betrayal, on the one side, and disillusion, on the other side, that is the central subject of the *Romanzo*. The adolescents of Bassani suffer from a peculiar trauma, that is, the trauma of failed assimilation which occurred to many Jews in Italy. With regard to the particular situation of the Jews of Ferrara, Bassani explains; "The real tragedy of the Ferrarese Jews, and of the most part of the Italian Jews, may be that of having been, as bourgeois, involved, at the beginning, with Fascism, and at the end without after all knowing why, in the nothing of the Nazi extermination camps"[114].

Finally, with the *Romanzo* Bassani leaves what may be called a "document of ambiguity". The marginal Jew, whom we mentioned at the beginning as the protagonist of Bassani's stories, lives in a cradle of ambiguity. He is animated by constant contradictions: repulsion and attachment to his Jewish origin; fear and love of diversity; separateness from and belonging to his native town. Ferrara is always the background, ready to evoke either painful memories or moments of happiness. Bruno defines Ferrara as a "common prison and ghetto"[115]; immediately after, in the same context, Clelia Trotti recalls the educational experience of the cell. "The truth is that the places where one has cried, where one has suffered, and where one has found the internal resources for hoping and resisting, are just the most beloved ones"[116].

Conclusion

What I have tried to demonstrate in my work is that the 'Romance of Ferrara' by Bassani should be considered in its entirety, in the sum of all the stories and novels contained. Although any of them has its autonomy, their unification within the same text corresponds to the author's specific intent: that of depicting the situation of the Jews of Ferrara under Fascism. In this sense, the *Romanzo* constitutes not just a novel, a fictional text, but a true document. According to the etymological meanings of this term, in fact, the document is at once a teaching, a warning and a written proof[117]. Such reading has allowed me to make what I hope is a fruitful confrontation between the testimony of a novelist and the recent historical debate on Italian anti-Semitism. It may perhaps be useful for interpreting others literary texts and raising other questions.

Notes

1. Paola Di Cori is Professor of History at the University of Turin. In relation to Italian anti-Semitism, she has written 'Le leggi antisemite' (The anti-Semitic laws), summarising the historiographical debate in Italy, which is collected in the volume *I luoghi della memoria* (The places of memory), Laterza, Roma, 1996 (p. 463–476).

2. Guia Risari: 'Jean Améry. Il risentimento come morale' (Resentment as Morals), University of Milan, (Dic. 1995). My thesis in Moral Philosophy is a philosophical analysis of the term resentment from Nietzsche to Jean Améry, passing through Scheler, Weber, Freud, Adorno and the Holocaust literature. See G. Risari: 'Il paradosso di un non-non ebreo', *QOL*, n. 64, 1996.

3. I am referring specifically to the work by Bauman, entitled *Modernity and Holocaust*, Polity Press, Cambridge, 1989.

4. D. Laub, S. Felman: *Testimony: Crisis of Witnessing in Literature, Psychoanalysis and History*, Routledge, New York-London, 1992.

5. J. E. Young: *Writing and Rewriting the Holocaust*, Indiana University Press, Bloomington, Indianapolis, 1988 (p. 6).

6. Giorgio Romano is a literary critic who has studied the Jewish element in Italian literature. He holds that in Italy this element is neither recurrent nor openly expressed. He attributes this silence to a sort of anxiety, on the Jewish part, about describing their environment. So he assumes that the only criterion for deciding whether or not a text of Italian literature has a Jewish element is its subject. Romano's study, although partly superseded, remains an excellent introduction to this topic. G. Romano: *Ebrei nella letteratura italiana* (The Jews in Italian literature), Carucci, Roma, 1978.

7. On this proposal, Radcliff-Umstead writes in his study on Bassani: "In his narrative writings, Bassani attempts to transcend the nightmare events of recent history by contemplating his characters and their forcibly closed world as if above and outside temporal bounds". D. Radcliff-Umstead: *The Exile into Eternity*, Associated University Press, London and Toronto, 1987 (p. 23).

8. M. Schneider: *Vengeance of the Victim*, University of Minnesota Press, Minneapolis, 1986, (p. 64).

9. This has seemed essential to me, considering the lack of familiarity of the English-speaking reader with the author and the whole Romance. Until now, in fact, the following four books by Bassani have been translated into English: *The Garden of the Finzi-Continis* (1989), *Behind the Door* (1997), *The Heron* (1993), *The Smell of Hay* (1996), all published by Paperback Quarter, London.

10. The poetry of Bassani has never been translated into English. Considering the difficulty of the

task, my translations try to respect the sense, more than the rhythm of the poems, giving prose versions of Bassani's originals. (An epoch dies, another is already here, completely new and innocent. However, I know, I will not be able to live this one also, but turned eternally backwards, to look in the direction of the time just passed, as I am indifferent to anything except what my life really was before and what kind of person I was.) G. Bassani: 'Muore un'epoca', in *In Rima e senza* (*With and without rhyme*), Mondadori, Milano, 1982 (p. 251).

11. *Il Corriere Padano* (*The Po-Journal*) was a Fascist newspaper, founded by the Fascist leader of Ferrara, Italo Balbo in 1925. Although it was the expression of the Ferrarese Fascism, its literary page allowed an almost complete freedom of expression. Here were published not only the first stories of Bassani, but also those of Antonioni and translations from Joyce, Eliot, Valéry. Anna Folli has edited an anthology of the literary activity of *Il Corriere*, which finally closed in April 1945. See A. Folli: *Vent'anni di cultura ferrarese* (Twenty years of Ferrarese Culture), Pàtron, Bologna, 1979, vol. I–II.

12. One of his students, Paolo Ravenna, remembers the enlightening lessons of Bassani, when the young graduate talked of authors never mentioned in the anthologies and showed another side of Italian culture. "Bassani led us out from the dark circle around us (...) Bassani was with us also in preparing us and the other students to a sort for self-defence against fear, against a complex of victimisation (...)". P. Ravenna: 'Bassani, insegnante negli anni '30', in *Bassani e Ferrara. Le intermittenze del cuore* (*Bassani and Ferrara. The gaps of the heart*), by A. Chiappini, G. Venturini, Gabriele Corbo Ed., Ferrara, 1995 (p. 95).

13. Bassani hints at his experience quite rarely in some poems and interviews. Another testimony of his imprisonment is given through his correspondence from the prison. See G. Bassani: 'Da una prigione' (From a prison) and 'Pagine di un diario ritrovato' (Pages of a rediscovered diary), in *Al di là del cuore* (*Beyond the Heart*), Mondadori, Milano, 1984 (pp. 9–55).

14. A cell atrophy has affected Bassani since about 1987. For other bibliographical details, see E. Siciliano: 'La memoria offesa' (The injured memory), *La Repubblica*, 8 lug. 1989 (p. 3).

15. G. Bassani: 'Caduta dell'amicizia', in A. Folli: *Vent'anni di cultura ferrarese*, op. cit., pp. 53–57 (p. 54–55).

16. P. P. Pasolini: *Descrizioni di descrizioni* (*Descriptions of descriptions*), Einaudi, Torino, pp. 262–266 (p. 264–265).

17. G. Cattaneo: 'Il Romanzo di Ferrara', in A. Sempoux: *Il Romanzo di Ferrara*, Louvaine, La-Neuve, Louvain, 1988 (pp. 27–40). This text is a collection of several essays, presented at the Department of Italian of Louvain, during a round table on Bassani.

18. Ada Neiger is a literary critic who has particularly studied the relations between Italian and Jewish traditions within the context of literature. To Bassani, she has devoted a whole book: *Bassani e il mondo ebraico* (*Bassani and the Jewish world*), Loffredo, Milano, 1983.

19. A. Dolfi: *Le forme del sentimento* (*The shapes of feelings*), Liviana, Padova, 1981.

20. G. Bassani: 'Laggiù in fondo al corridoio' (Way Down at the End of the Corridor), in *Il Romanzo di Ferrara*, Mondadori, Milano, 1980, pp. 729–734 (p. 732).

21. Bassani disputes more than once with the ideological and naïve conception of Neo-realism which combines individuals and events as if they were two simple realities which interconnect. With regard to the chronicle, therefore, Bassani holds that the record of historical facts, dates and names is nothing in itself. Only the grasping of a sense, of the spirit dominating a certain period, transforms the negligible list into history. In underlining the value of the spirit over the mere fact, Bassani shows himself to be the heir not only of Croce's historicism, but also of its fundamental idealistic trend.

22. F. Camon: *Il mestiere di scrittore* (*The skill of the writer*), Garzanti, Milano, 1973 (p. 66).

23. This is especially true when Bassani deals with tragic and bloody events, such as deportation and murders. We will analyse later the meaning of this silence.

24. Gian Carlo Ferretti has been perhaps the most representative leader of this trend. For him,

Bassani expresses a dissent between moral and literary suggestion, typical of his generation. "The more the writer (...) tries to get a historical, critical meaningfulness, the more the elegy and the myths of the past hold him again in their consolatory world". G. C. Ferretti: *Letteratura e ideologia* (Literature and ideology) (p. 59).

25. E. Siciliano: 'Bassani o l'anima della storia' (Bassani or the spirit of history), in G. Grana: *Novecento*, Mazzorati, Milano, 1979, pp. 6697–6707 (p. 6702).

26. Radcliff-Umstead writes: "(...) the spiritual movement of Bassani's narrative writings leads his tormented characters beyond the time of history and chronicle to an eternal literary world". D. Radcliff-Umstead: *The Exile into Eternity*, Associated University Press, London-Toronto, 1987 (p. 36).

27. A. Dolfi: op. cit. (p. 35).

28. G. Varanini: 'L'arte di Giorgio Bassani', in *Il Romanzo di Ferrara*, op. cit. (pp. 65–79). The literary commentator is also the author of a brief monograph on the writer: 'Bassani', *Il Castoro* 46, La Nuova Italia, Firenze, 1975.

29. G. Bassani, in *Il mestiere di scrittore*, op. cit. (pp. 59–60).

30. (The big old Fascists of Ferrara get older; some of those who in '39 seemed not to recognise me any more, cross the road and throw, as they did with Geo, their arms around my neck. Irresistible gaffeurs, they sigh: "Oh you", and suggest, after the painful slap on the left shoulder, the domestic agape, that finally allows the monumental Catholic mummy, coming from Bologna or Rovigo, and the extra-blond, spotless teenagers, who tea in the dining room, to meet me once and for all. Me, the ex-school-mate so skilful, the skilful novelist, the president... They seem to suggest, in the meantime, "Come on, stop it, don't you see that you, you too, are a zombie? And then, sorry – they continue, just equal yet to the engineer Marcello Rimini, to the rabbi Doctor Viterbo – how, without us, could you have gathered together your stories and the necessary financial support, and so on? After all, shit, you could even start to consider us also almost as half..." Race-mates? You quoque? Almost like half-cousins? No, slow down! How the shit is it possible? Before that, my dears, we have to die). G. Bassani: 'Gli ex fascistoni di Ferrara', in *In rima e senza*, op. cit. (pp. 135–137).

31. Alexander Stille is the son of two Russian Jews who emigrated to Italy in 1922, and then, in 1941, finally to America. The surname of the author derives from the pseudonym (in German, silence) that his father adopted after 1938 to work as a journalist. Against a history concentrated on politics and diplomacy, he aims to record how the Italian Jews actually lived under Fascism. "With the exception of Giorgio Bassani's novel 'The Garden of the Finzi-Continis', there was no book that conveyed the paradoxical quality of Jewish life in Fascist Italy (...)". A. Stille: *Benevolence and Betrayal*, Jonathan Cape, London, 1991 (p. 12).

32. A. Milano: *Storia degli ebrei in Italia* (*History of the Jews in Italy*), Einaudi, Torino, 1992 (p. 693).

33. Ibid. (p. XXIII).

34. It is useful to recall that Italy has the infamous distinction in Europe of being the site of the first ghetto, that of Venice in 1516, and of the last one, that of Rome closed only in 1870.

35. Stuart Hugues, Professor of History at the University of San Diego, California, has dedicated his book to eight Italian Jewish writers, among whom also Bassani. S. Hugues: *Prisoners of Hope*, Harvard University Press, Cambridge-Massachussetts-London, 1996 (p. 9).

36. In 1873, the Jew Isacco Pesaro Maurogonato had been suggested as new Minister of Finance. His election was opposed by the liberal deputy from Venice, Francesco Pasqualigo. It was quite rare that a liberal and not a clerical should do this. Pasqualigo himself specified that it was not for religious reasons, but for "exclusively political motives". The double nationality of the Jews, their being a state within a state, could not guarantee a post which was in its essence nationalist.

37. For the relation between the Italian Jews and Fascism, see E. Collotti: *Fascismo, fascismi*

(*Fascism, fascisms*), Sansoni, Firenze, 1989. The author also explains the main differences between the Italian Jews of the peninsula and those of Libya.

38. Renzo De Felice is one of the first Italian scholars, in the second post-war period to deal with the Fascist discrimination and persecution of the Jews. Thanks to him, a whole historiographical school has arisen in Italy, devoted to the study of this question. Nevertheless, his approach to the problem has been criticised, basically for two reasons. He emphasises more the Italian attitude towards Jews, almost ignoring the Jewish party; he assumes that, prior to the March on Rome, anti-Semitism was virtually non existent in Italy. R. De Felice: *Gli Ebrei sotto il fascismo* (*The Jews under Fascism*), Einaudi, Milano, 1961.

    For a brief history of the historiographical trends on this subject, see M. Michalis: 'The 'Duce' and the Jews. An Assessment of the Literature on Italian Jewry under Fascism', in M. R. Marrus: *The Nazi Holocaust*, Meckler, Westport-London, 1989, vol. 4 (pp. 191–216).

39. L. Poliakov, J. Sabille: *Gli Ebrei sotto l'occupazione italiana* (*The Jews under Italian occupation*), Ed. di Comunità, Milano, 1956 (p. 6).

40. Ibid. (p. 5).

41. S. Zuccotti: *The Italians and the Holocaust*, Peter Halban, London, 1987 (p. 275).

42. L. Picciotto Fargion: *Il libro della memoria* (*The book of memory*), Mursia, Milano, 1991 (p. 836). In this book, the author records all the names and where possible the fate of the Jewish victims of Fascism in Italy. Thanks to an accurate and long research in various archives, she gives some precise data: of a total population of 35,260, present in Italy and in the Dodecanese, 8566 Jews were deported and 303 killed. The survivors numbered 1090: respectively, 179 of the 1820 arrested in the Greek Islands, 830 of the 6746 captured in Italy. Forty-four trains left Italy from September 1943 to August 1945.

43. On the idea of the 'Fascist man', as the keyword for a complete, cultural homologation, see M. L. Leeden: 'The Evolution of Italian Fascist Antisemitism', in M. R. Marrus: *The Nazi Holocaust*, op. cit. (pp. 240–254).

44. The above mentioned historian Enzo Collotti specialised in the study of the totalitarian systems. Two points of his work are especially important: (1) the existence of many forms, or better degrees of Fascism; (2) the tendency of Fascism to overlap with Nazism, which is just the final and extreme phase of Fascism. E. Collotti: *Fascismo, fascismi*, op., cit.

45. For the various meanings of the Fascist notion of race, which is at once 'people', 'spiritual community', 'civilisation' and 'Latin origin', see G. Bernardini: 'The Origins and Development of Racial Anti-Semitism', in M. R. Marrus: *The Nazi Holocaust*, op. cit. (pp. 217–239).

46. D. Bidussa: 'I caratteri 'propri' dell'antisemitismo italiano' (The peculiar elements of Italian anti-Semitism), in *La menzogna della razza* (*The lie of the race*), Grafis Ed., Bologna, 1994 (pp. 113–124).

47. D. Bidussa: *Il mito del buon Italiano* (*The myth of the Good Italian*), Il Saggiatore, Milano, 1994 (p. 67).

48. Michele Sarfatti has recently devoted a whole book to the analysis of the different versions of the Racial Laws, elaborated by Mussolini. They represent nine months, from February to November 1938, of hard and planned work. It does not matter whether Mussolini himself was or was not an anti-Semite, more cynical than insane. For Sarfatti, the concrete acts, the laws, are more significant than any public statement of the dictator, which is just propaganda. The historian's conclusion is that the Italian anti-Semitic legislation was a coherent and original model for persecuting the Jews. In some respects, it was even harsher than the German one. M. Sarfatti: *Mussolini contro gli ebrei* (Mussolini against the Jews), Ed. Silvio Zamorani, Einaudi, Torino, 1994.

49. S. Urso: 'La persecuzione degli ebrei in Italia' (The persecution of the Jews in Italy), in *Studi Storici*, Ed. Dedalo. ott.-dic. 1994, pp. 1153–1165 (p. 1164–1165).

50. Raul Hilberg, in his latest version of *The Destruction of the European Jews*, seems to be well informed of the recent data and debates. He also stresses the autonomy of Italy from Germany. Despite this, he starts by saying: "(...) the relationship between Jews and Italians had progressed to a point which made Italian persecution of the Jews psychologically as well as administratively difficult". R. Hilberg: *The Destruction of the European Jews*, Holmes & Meier, New York, London, 3 vol., 1985, vol. II, pp. 660–679 (p. 661).

51. The historian Tony Kushner, in denouncing the persistence of prejudice in the Liberal countries, rightly distinguishes between a generous behaviour and an opportunistic one. But at the same time, he provides the already discussed myth with a too generous parallel. "The cases of Italy and Denmark, perhaps the most important in terms of saving the Jews in the war, were the results of Italian and Danish self-esteem rather than philosemitism or opposition to antisemitism (...)". T. Kusher: *The Holocaust and the Liberal Imagination*, Basic Blackwell, Oxford, 1994.

52. P. R. Corner: *Il fascismo a Ferrara. 1915–1925 (The fascism in Ferrara)*, Laterza, Roma-Bari, 1974 (p. 155).

53. From 1534 to 1538, the Duke Ercole II addressed a series of letters, praising the Jews wherever persecution occurred. In 1532, the Jews from Bohemia were invited, in 1540, arrived the Jews banished from Milanese Dukedom and 1541, it was the turn of the Jews, expelled from the Kingdom of Naples. Also some Marranos escaping the Inquisition were invited to Ferrara. See A. Milano: *Storia degli Ebrei in Italia*, op. cit.

54. Famous was the salon of the Abravanels, which was the true cenacle for Jews and Christians. In Renaissance Ferrara, Jews were also allowed to attend the University and to take doctoral degrees. In this town, Azharia de' Rossi, the greatest Hebrew scholar of this period, settled, after his expulsion from the Dukedom of Mantua. For a better picture of the Renaissance atmosphere, see D. B. Ruderman: *The World of a Renaissance Jew*, Cincinnati, 1981.

55. As an example of the success of Fascism in Ferrara, in March 1921, the Roman Fascists numbered 1480; in Milan, the alleged cradle of Fascism, they were 6,000, while in Ferrara they reached the number of 7000. In the same period, 6 out of 17 landowners registered to the Fascio were Jewish. See P. Corner: *Le origini del fascismo a Ferrara*, op. cit.

56. Ibid. (p. 141).

57. B. Pincherle: 'Gli ebrei a Ferrara dal Fascismo alla liberazione' (The Jews of Ferrara from fascism to the liberation), in F. Loperfido: *Renzo Bonfiglioli. Ebreo Ferrarese*, Gabriele Corbo Ed., Ferrara, 1989 (pp. 67–92). This book is mainly a commemoration dedicated to a Jew, Renzo Ravenna, persecuted for his anti-Fascism. He was a landowner and lawyer who refused to join the Fascist party. For this reason, he could never practise law and was later imprisoned and exiled from Ferrara. The book *Renzo Bonfiglioli* is also an effort to stress the contribution of the Ferrarese Jewry to the Resistance movement.

58. Franco Schönheit, together with his mother and father, was deported from Ferrara to Fossoli in February 1944. The Schönheit family succeeded in surviving mainly thanks to their status as half-Jewish, which prolonged their stay in Fossoli. As the last Jews of Fossoli, they were sent to Buchenwald, not to Auschwitz. Franco records the responsibility of the Italian police in arresting the Ferrarese Jews. A. Stille: *Benevolence and Betrayal*, op. cit., pp. 279–314, 343–349 (p. 285).

59. Pincherle sustains that also few important Fascists showed openly their disagreement. Italo Balbo, for example, after the enactment of the Laws, invited his friend Ravenna to the best restaurant in Ferrara. He and the others who showed off their dissent were labelled 'Pietisti', for being sympathetic with the Jews. See *Renzo Bonfiglioli*, op. cit.

60. Once again, this step has been differently interpreted. What we have called the traditional historiographical school held that the Italian government wanted to save the Jews from the accusation of parasitism. On the other hand, the new historiographical trend reminds that the

State itself had provoked the accusation, excluding Jews from military service. So the only aim of the measure was, in fact, to humiliate the Jews. For other details, see *1938. A 50'anni dalle leggi razziali* (*50 years after the racial laws*), ed. by Consiglio Regionale della Toscana, 1938.

61.   The number of the victims is revised by Liliana Piggiotto Fargion, who specifies that 71 Ferrarese Jews died in the concentration camp and 11 died from a direct persecution. Five were the survivors from the concentration camp. See L. Picciotto Fargion: *Il Libro della memoria*, op. cit.

        The total given by the historian is in contrast with that the *Judaica Encyclopaedia*, which reports about 200 deported. See 'Ferrara', in *Judaica Encyclopaedia*, Israel, 16 vol., 1971, vol. 6 (pp. 1231–1235).

62.   Preserve me, I pray you, exclusive God of the oldest, from the bitter and joyful leisure of abandoning myself – as happened to my father from about '30 till at least '38 and the Racial laws – in the arms of the Italian moderate class, eternally treacherous, blameless as always, at once Fascist and Innocent. Rescue me, I beg you, as you can, from their sweet females, from the promises of their intact, almost eternal, dear Catholic-rural jargons, from everything I know that I most love and most detest in the world, most adore and abhor.

63.   Some interpreters have even seen in the figure of Bruno the double of Bassani. Both of them were good tennis players and were engaged to Christian girls. Also common to both is their passion for literature and their sudden adhesion to leftist ideals. On the other hand, Bruno can be seen rather as the hidden, the alternate, perhaps the dark side of the writer (and it may not be a coincidence that Bruno in Italian means 'brown'). From the physical point of view, in fact, they are opposite: Bassani was blond and short, provided with strong legs and an athletic physique; Bruno is more similar to the stereotypical Jew of the ghetto: dark hair, tall but with a very pale complexion and a skinny body. See M. Schneider: *Vengeance of the Victim*, op. cit.

64.   A. Neiger: *Bassani e il mondo ebraico*, op. cit.

65.   G. Bassani: 'Due favole' (Two tales), in *Il Romanzo di Ferrara*, op. cit., pp. 669–672 (p. 669).

66.   Ibid. (p. 671–672).

67.   G. Bassani: *La passeggiata prima di cena* (*The Walk before Dinner*), ibid., pp. 45–66 (p. 60).

68.   A record of the local Jewish-Italian jargon is present in 'Argon' by Primo Levi. In this case the author explicitly says that the function of the Jewish-Torinese was to speak of delicate subjects in front of the Gentiles. P. Levi: 'Argon', in *Il sistema periodico* (*The Periodic Table*), Einaudi Torino, 1969 (pp. 1–21).

69.   M. Schneider: *Vengeance of the Victim*, op. cit. (p. 71).

70.   G. Bassani: *La passeggiata prima di cena*, op. cit. (p. 63).

71.   Ibid. (p. 53).

72.   Here is very clearly expressed the sexual curiosity and fear for the 'Jewish body'. For a description of the prejudices, related to the various parts of this mysterious body, see S. Gilman: *The Jewish Body*, Routledge, New York and London, 1991.

73.   For a treatment of this theme – the exotic sensuality of the Jewess – and a wider discussion of what is Orientalism, see the study of Edward W. Said: *Orientalism*, Routledge & Kegan Paul, London and Henley, 1978.

74.   G. Bassani: *Dietro la porta* (Behind the Door), op. cit., pp. 451–543 (p. 526). At that time, Bassani was 16 years old. The high school that he attended specialised in classical studies, in fact, start with two years called 'gymnasium' (IV-V), followed by three further years of 'liceo' (I-III).

75.   Ibid. (p. 453).

76.   Ibid. (p. 523).

77.   In this respect, the hostility of Cattolica corresponds quite well to the religious anti-Semitism, or better the Christian one. For the responsibility of Christian theology in diffusing the negative image of the Jew as Devil, see what Hyam Maccoby has written in *Judas Iscariot and*

     the *Myth of Jewish Evil*, Free Press, London, 1992.

78. G. Bassani: *Dietro la porta*, op. cit. (p. 472).

79. G. Bassani, *Gli occhiali d'oro* (*The Golden-rimmed Eyeglasses*), ibid., pp. 165–245 (p. 226).

80. G. Bassani: *Il Giardino dei Finzi-Contini* (*The Garden of the Finzi-Continis*), ibid., pp. 249–450 (p. 291).

81. There are in Bassani's accounts of historical events some mistakes, or better, voluntary imprecisions. Five and not just one was the number of Ferrarese Jews to survive the deportation. The Ferrarese Jews deported were 87 and not 187. Moreover, the Jews shot in Via Mazzini were four out of 14 and not four out of eight. The function of this increase in the 'quantity' of violence is to enhance the dramatic quality of the events.

82. G. Bassani: *Gli ultimi anni di Clelia Trotti* (*The Last Years of Clelia Trotti*), ibid., pp. 97–133 (p. 108).

83. A. Spinette: 'Il cerchio inquieto' (The restless circle), in A. Sempoux: *Il romanzo di Ferrara*, op. cit. (pp. 81–84). His observations parallel those of another critic, Giuso Oddo De Stefanis, who has stressed the metaphoric quality of Bassani's writings. See G. Oddo De Stefanis: B*assani dentro il cerchio delle sue mura* (*Bassani within the circle of his walls*), Longo, Ravenna, 1981.

84. A. Dolfi: *Le forme del sentimento*, op. cit. (p. 83).

85. G. Bassani: *Lidia Mantovani*, op. cit., pp. 9-43 (p. 39).

86. Renato Bertacchini is perhaps the first Italian literary critic who has stressed the 'Jewish element' in Bassani's writing. He even spoke of "the semitism of Bassani". See R. Bertacchini: 'Appunti sul semitismo di Bassani' (Notes on Bassani's Semitism), in *Convivium*, anno XXVIII, marzo-aprile 1952, n. 2 (pp. 179–192). For the explanation of Bassani's anti-Fascist prose, see R. Bertacchini: 'Giorgio Bassani', in G. Grana: *Novecento*, op. cit. (pp. 6667–6718).

87. A. Dolfi: *Le forme del sentimento*, op. cit. (p. 9).

88. The so-called 'novels of the self' of Bassani are those where the author appears as a narrating voice and speaks in the first person. So, they are the novels written after the five stories of *Within the Walls*: *The Golden-rimmed Eyeglasses, The Garden* and *Behind the Door. The Heron*, where the third person reappears, is a borderline case.

89. With this expression, the author refers to what he interprets as the artistic process of Bassani, that is, the creation of a literary Limbo where the vanished world is immortalised. D. Radcliff-Umsted: *Exile into Eternity*, Associated University Press, London and Toronto, 1987 (p. 146).

90. G. Bassani: *Il Giardino dei Finzi Contini,* op. cit. (p. 396).

91. The expression 'stigma of difference', as a sign of Jewish diversity comes from Zygmund Bauman's 'Strangers: The social Construction of Universality and Particularity', in *Telos*, n. 78, 1988-89 (pp. 1–36). In this essay, the Jew is representative of the stranger who 'comes to stay' and constitutes a perennial challenge for the environment.

     For a parallel between the conditions of Jews and homosexuals in Bassani, see A. Neiger: 'Modelli di difformità' (Models of deformity), in *L'ebraismo nella letteratura italiana del '900* (*The Jewishness in the 20th century Italian literature*), ed. by M. Carlà, L. de Angelis, Palumbo, Palermo, 1995 (pp. 101–106).

92. Stanley Eskin has defined Jewishness and sexuality as the central themes of 'The Garden' and 'Behind the Door'. For the critic, in fact, sexuality is the principal means to face the identity problem. See S. G. Eskin:'Sex and Jewishness', in *Midstream*, n. 6, June/July, 1973 (pp. 71–75).

93. Ada Neiger suggests how Bassani has projected his own trauma of rejection, typical of the 'marginal Jew', to an object of desire, sacred as well as illegal, the Christian-Aryan woman. A. Neiger: *Bassani e il mondo ebraico*, op. cit.

94. From this point of view, also, the names of these two characters are meaningful. Sciagura, the leader of the Fascist massacre, means in Italian literally 'calamity'. On the other hand, the

name of Barillari, the passive witness, recalls a famous mark of pasta (Barilla). Hence, he would represent the typical Italian.

95. C. Varese: 'Spazio e tempo del 'Giardino dei Finzi-Contini' a 'L'airone'' (Space and time from 'The Garden' to 'The Heron''), in A. Chiappini, G. Venturi: *Le intermittenze del cuore*, op. cit., 1995 (pp. 17–27).
96. G. Bassani, in *Il mestiere di scrittore*, op. cit.
97. G. Bassani, in *Le forme del sentimento*, op. cit. (p. 90).
98. G. Bassani: *Laggiù in fondo al corridoio*, op. cit., (p. 729).
99. G. Bassani: *Altre notizie su Bruno Lattes* (*More News on Bruno Lattes*), ibid. (p. 679).
100. G. Bassani: 'Il muro di cinta' (The enclosure wall), in *Le storie ferraresi*, Einaudi, Torino, 1960, pp. 7–11 (p. 7).
101. G. Bassani: *Altre notizie su Bruno Lattes*, op. cit. (p. 677–678).
102. D. Radcliff-Umstead: *Exile into Eternity*, op. cit. (p. 74).
103. G. Bassani, in *Le forme del sentimento*, op. cit. (p. 91).
104. This opinion is expressed by Giovanna Finocchiaro, who explains the presence of so many adolescents in Bassani by the fact that the writer himself, at the time of anti-Semitic legislation, was an adolescent too. G. Finocchiaro: 'Adolescenti di Bassani' (Adolescents in Bassani), in A. Sempoux: *Il romanzo di Ferrara*, op. cit. (pp. 41–61).
105. G. Bassani: *Laggiù in fondo al corridoio*, op. cit., (p. 734).
106. R. Bertacchini: *Giorgio Bassani*, op cit. (p. 6682).
107. G. Bassani: *Le parole preparate*, op. cit. (p. 385).
108. See, for example, Haron Rosenfeld: *A Double Dying*, Indiana University Press, Bloomington, 1980. This work quotes only *The Garden of the Finzi-Continis* in the final bibliography regarding the fictional novel. The book by S. Dekoven Ezrahi, instead, contains a brief reference to Bassani in a chapter on 'The Holocaust Mythologized'. See *By Words Alone*, University of Chicago Press, 1980 (pp. 172–173).
109. I am referring to Tina Matarrese, a literary critic who has especially analysed Bassani's use of language in 'Bassani e la lingua del Romanzo' (Bassani and the language of the Romance), in A. Chiappini, G.Venturi: *Le intermittenze del cuore*, op. cit. (pp. 47-63).
110. A parallel may be done with the metaphors used by Celan in *Todesfuge*. The verbal material of his poem, in fact, comes from the desrupted world of the concentration camp. For a detailed study of the poetry and life of Celan, see J. Felstiner: *Paul Celan, Poet, Survivor, Jew*, Yale University Press, New-Haven and London, 1995.
111. G. Bassani: *Il Giardino dei Finzi-Contini*, op. cit. (p. 278).
112. G. Bassani: *Gli occhiali d'oro*, op. cit. (p. 292).
113. G. Bassani: *Il Giardino dei Finzi-Contini*, op. cit. (p. 171).
114. G. Bassani: *Le parole preparate*, op. cit. (p. 387).
115. G. Bassani: *Gli ultimi anni di Clelia Trotti*, op. cit. (p. 122).
116. Ibid. (p. 130).
117. See the voice 'document' in *The Oxford Dictionary*, ed. by J. A. Simpson and E. S. C. Weiner, Clarendon Press, Oxford, 20 vol., 1989, vol. IV (p. 916).

Bibliography

Primary Sources

Works by Bassani
Il Romanzo di Ferrara, Mondadori, Milano, 1980:
> *Dentro le mura* ('Lidia Mantovani' – 'La passeggiata prima di cena' – 'Gli ultimi anni di Clelia Trotti' – 'Una notte del '43'); Gli occhiali d'oro; Il giardino dei Finzi-Contini; Dietro la porta; L'airone; L'odore del fieno; Due favole; Altre notizie su Bruno Lattes; Ravenna; Les neiges d'antan; Tre apologhi; Laggiù in fondo al corridoio

Le storie ferraresi, Einaudi Torino, 1960:
> Il muro di cinta; Lidia Mantovani; La passeggiata prima di cena; Gli ultimi anni di Clelia Trotti; Una notte del '43

In rima e senza, Mondadori, Milano, 1982:
> Storie dei poveri amanti; Te Lucis ante; Traducendo; Epitaffio; In gran segreto

Al di là del cuore, Mondadori, Milano, 1984

Secondary Sources

Criticism On Bassani
Bertacchini, Renato: Appunti sul semitismo di Bassani, in *Convivium*, anno XXVIII, marzo-aprile 1952, n. 2 (pp. 179–192)

Camon, Ferdinando: *Il mestiere di scrittore,* Garzanti, Milano, 1973

Chiappini, Aldo; Venturini, Giorgio: *Le intermittenze del cuore*, Gabriele Corbo, Ferrara, 1995

Dolfi, Anna: *Le forme del sentimento. Prosa e poesia in Giorgio Bassani*, Liviana Ed., Padova, 1981

Eskin, Stanley, G.: Sex and Jewishness in Giorgio Bassani, in *Midstream*, n. 6, June/July 1973 (pp. 71–75)

Ferretti, Gian Carlo: *Letteratura e ideologia. Bassani, Cassola, Pasolini*, Ed. Riuniti, Roma, 1978

Folli, Anna: *Vent'anni di cultura ferrarese*, Pàtron, Bologna, 1979, vol. I-II

Goldman, Annie: Le jardinier de Ferrare, in *L'Arche*, n. 318–319, Sept–Oct. 1983 (pp. 178–181)

Grana, Gianni: *Novecento. I contemporanei*, Mazzorati, Milano, 1979, vol. VII, BASSANI (pp. 6667–6718)

Hugues, Stuart: *Prisoners of Hope*, Harvard University Press, Cambridge-Massachussetts-London, 1996

Lombardini, Olga: Giorgio Bassani, in *Narratori italiani del secondo '900*, Longo, Ravenna, 1981 (pp. 58–66)

Neiger, Ada: *Bassani e il mondo ebraico*, Loffredo, Milano, 1983

Neiger, Ada: Modelli di difformità, in *L'ebraismo nella letteratura italiana del '900*, ed. by M. Carlà and L. De Angelis, Palumbo, Palermo, 1995 (pp. 101–106)

Oddo De Stefanis, Giuso: *Bassani dentro il cerchio delle sue mura*, Longo, Ravenna, 1981

Pasolini, Pier Paolo: *Descrizioni di descrizioni*, Einaudi, Torino, 1979 (pp. 262-266)

Pautasso, Sergio: Alle Fondamenta della cattedrale, in *Il laboratorio dello scrittore*, La Nuova Italia, Firenze, 1981 (pp. 53–64)

Radcliff-Umstead, Douglas: *The Exile into Eternity*, Associated University Press, London, Toronto, 1987

Romano, Giorgio: *Ebrei nella letteratura italiana*, Carucci, Roma, 1979

Russi, Antonio: Giorgio Bassani, in *La narrativa italiana dal Neosperimentalismo alla Neoavanguardia*, Lucarini ed., Roma, 1983 (pp. 78–102)

Schneider, Marilyn: *Vengeance of the Victim*, University of Minnesota Press, Minneapolis, 1986

Sempoux, André: *Il romanzo di Ferrara*, Louvaine-La Neuve, Louvain, 1988

History of Ferrara

Bonfil., Robert: *Jewish life in Renaissance Italy*, University Press of California, Berkeley, London, 1994

Corner, Paul R.: *Il fascismo a Ferrara. 1915–1925*, Laterza, Roma-Bari, 1974

Judaica Enciclopedia: *Ferrara*, Israel, 16 vol., 1971, vol. 6 (pp. 1231–1235)

Loperfido, Francesco: *Renzo Bonfiglioli. Ebreo ferrarese*, Gabriele Corbo Ed., Ferrara, 1989

Milano, Attilio: *Storia degli ebrei in Italia*, Einaudi, Torino, 1992

Pincherle, Bruno: *Il fascismo a Ferrara. 1915–1925*, Laterza, Roma-Bari, 1974

Ruderman, David B.: *The World of a Renaissance Jews*, University Press, Cincinnati, 1981

Italian Fascism and Anti-Semitism

Bidussa, Davide: *La menzogna della razza*, Grafis Ed., Bologna, 1994

Bidussa, Davide: *Il mito del bravo italiano*, Il Saggiatore, Milano, 1994

Barford, Wanda V.: Ffijji d'Adamo, in *The Jewish Quarterly*, Winter 1993 (pp. 27–28)

Camera dei Deputati: La legislazione antiebraica in Italia, *Atti del Convegno nel cinquantenario delle leggi razziali*, Roma, 1989

Caracciolo, Nicola: *Gli Ebrei e l'Italia durante la guerra 1940–45*, Bonacci, Roma, 1986

Collotti, Enzo: *Fascismo, Fascismi*, Sansoni, Firenze, 1989

Consiglio Regionale della Toscana: *1938. A cinquant'anni dalle leggi razziali*, 1988

De Felice, Renzo: *Gli Ebrei sotto il fascismo*, Mursia, Milano, 1991

Di Cori, Paola: Le leggi razziali, in *I luoghi della memoria*, Laterza, Roma, 1996 (pp. 463–476)

Gilbert, Peter: Italians in War-time, in *The Jewish Quarterly*, Winter 1993 (pp. 24–25)

Hilberg, Raul: *The Destruction of the European Jews*, Holmes & Meier, New York, London, 1985

Jesorum, Stefano: *Essere ebrei in Italia*, Longanesi, Milano, 1987

Marrus, Michael R.: *The Nazi Holocaust,* Meckler, Westport, London, 1989, vol. IV (pp. 191–254)

Molinari, Maurizio: *Ebrei in Italia: un problema d'identità*, Giuntina, Firenze, 1991

Picciotto Fargion, Liliana: *Il libro della memoria*, Mursia, Milano, 1991

Poliakov, Leòn; Sabille, Jacques: *Gli Ebrei sotto l'occupazione italiana*, Ed. di Comunità, Milano, 1956

Sarfatti, Michele: *Mussolini contro gli ebrei*, Ed. Silvio Zamorani, Torino, 1994

Stille, Alexander: *Benevolence and Betrayal*, Jonathan Cape, London, 1991

Urso, Simona: La persecuzione degli ebrei in Italia, in *Studi Storici*, Ed. Dedalo, ott.-dic. 1994 (pp. 1153–1165)

Zevi Tullia: Preface, in *Gardens and Ghettoes*, V. Mann ed., New York, 1989 (pp. XII–XIII)

Zuccotti, Susan: *The Italians and the Holocaust*, Peter Halban, London, 1987

Zuccotti, Susan: Noble Romans, in *The Jewish Quarterly*, Winter 1993 (pp. 26–27)

Stereotypes of the Jews

Adorno, Theodor W.; Horkheimer, Max: Dialectic of enlightenment, *Continuum*, New York, 1995

Alcalay, Ammiel: *After Jews and Arabs*, University of Minnesota Press, Minneapolis, 1993

Cheyette, Brian: *'Construction of the Jew' in English Literature and society: racial representation*, Cambridge University Press, 1993

Curtis, Michael: *Antisemitism in the Contemporary World*, Westview Press, Boulder and London, 1986

Deutscher, Isaac: *The non-Jewish Jew and other Essays*, Oxford University Press, 1968.

Felsenstein, Frank: *Anti-Semitic Stereotypes*, John Hopkins University Press, Baltimore-London, 1995

Fintz, Menascé, Esther: *L'ebreo errante. Metamorfosi di un mito (The wandering Jew, Metamorphosis of the Myth)*, Cisalpino, Milano, 1993

Garb, Tamar; Nochlin, Linda: *The Jew in the Text*, Thames and Hudson, New York and London, 1995

Gilman, Sander: *The Jewish Body*, Routledge, New York-London, 1991

Gilman, Sander: *Jewish Self-Hatred*, The John Hopkin University Press, Baltimore-London, 1986

Langmur, Gavin: *Toward a Definition of Antisemitism*, University of California Press, Los Angeles, 1990

Maccoby, Hyam: *Judas Iscariot and the Myth of Jewish evil*, Free Press, London, 1992

Macdonald, D.B.: *The Hebrew Philosophical Genius. A Vindication*, Princeton University Press, 1936.

Poliakov, Leon: *Histoire de l'antisemitism: 1945–1993*, Ed. Du Seuil, Paris, 1991

Said, Edward, W.: *Orientalism*, Routledge & Kegan Paul, London, Henley, 1978

Modernity and Assimilation

Altmann, Abraham: Moses Mendelssohn as the Archetypal German Jew, in *The Response to German Culture*, University Press of New England, Hanover, London, 1985, pp. 17–31

Altmann, Abraham: *Moses Mendelssohn. A Biographical Study*, The University of Alabama Press, 1973

Bach, Hans I.: *The German Jew. A Synthesis of Judaism and Western Civilisation*, Oxford University Press, 1984

Bauman, Zygmund: Exit Visas and Entry Tickets: Paradoxes of Jewish Assimilation, in *Telos*, N. 77, 1988 (pp. 45–77)

Bauman, Zygmund: *Modernity and Ambivalence*, Polity Press, Cambridge, 1993

Bauman, Zygmund: Strangers, in *Telos*, n. 78, 1988–89 (pp. 1–36)

Cesarani, David: *Citizenship, Nationality and Migration in Europe*, Routledge, London, New York, 1996

Cooper, Howard; Morrison, Paul: *Sense of Belonging: Dilemmas of British-Jewish Identity*, 1991

Deleuze, Gile; Guattari, Felix: *A Thousand Plateau. Capitalism and Schizophrenia*, The Athlone Press, London, 1988 (p. 291)

Felman, David: *Englishmen and Jews: English Political Culture 1840–1914* , 1994

Rose, Gillian: *Judaism and Modernity*, Blackwell, Oxford-Cambridge, 1993

Grosz, Elizabeth: Judaism and Exile: the Ethics of Otherness, in *New Formations*, n. 12, 1990 (pp. 77–88)

Hall, Stuart: Minimal Selves, in *Identity: The Real me*, London I CA Documents, 6, 1987 (pp. 44–46)

Katz, Jacob: *Emancipation and assimilation*, Gregg International Publishers Limited, Westmead, Farnborough, 1972

Katz, Jacob: *Out of ghetto,* Harvard University Press, Cambridge-Massachusetts, 1973.

Kleeblat, Norman: *Too Jewish?,* Rutgers University Press, 1993

Kochan, Lyonell: *The Jewish renaissance and some of its discontents*, Manchester University Press, 1992

Levinas, Emmanuel: *Difficult Freedom*, Baltimore, Johns Hopkins University Press, 1990

Mayer, A.: *The Origin of the Modern Jew*, Wayne University Press, Detroit, 1979

Mayer, R.: *A History of Modern Jewry. 1780–1815*, Vallentine, London, 1971

Mendes-Flohr, Paul R.; Reinharz, Jehuda: *The Jews in the Modern World: A Documentary History*, NY, 1980

Mosse, George L.: *German Jews Beyond Judaism*, Indiana University Press, Bloomington, 1985

Simmel, George: The Stranger (Der Fremde), in *Soziologie*, Duncker & Humblot, Munich, Leipzig (pp. 685–691)

Holocaust Literature

Adorno, Theodor W.: Commitment, (1961), in *The Essential Frankfurt School-Reader*, Basil Blackwell, Oxford, 1978 (pp. 300–318)

Adorno, Theodor W.: *Negative Dialectics*, Routledge, London, 1990

Alvarez, Al: *Beyond all this fiddle,* Penguin Press, London, 1968

Bauman, Zygmund: *Modernity and Holocaust,* Polity Press, Cambridge, 1989

Boyarin, James: *Storm from Paradise*, University of Minnesota Press, Minneapolis, 1992

Chevalier, Yves: *L'antisemitisme. Le Juif comme bouc émissaire*, Les Edition du Cerf, Paris, 1988

Dekoven, S. Ezrahi: "By Words Alone", University of Chicago Press, Chicago, 1980

Felstiner, John: *Paul Celan, Poet, Survivor, Jew*, Yale University Press, New Haven, CT, London, 1995

Friedlander, Saul: *Probing the Limits of Representation*, Harvard University Press, Cambridge, MA, London, 1992

Freud, Sigmund: Mourning and Melancholia, in *On Metapsychology*, vol. 11, Pellican Freud Library, 1984 (pp. 251–268)

Hartman, George: *Holocaust Remembrance: the Shapes of memory*, Blackwell, Cambridge, MA, London, 1994

Jabès, Edmond: *L'Enfer de Dant*, Cognac, Fata Morgana, 1991

Lang, Berel: *Act and Idea in the Nazi Genocide*, The University Chicago Press, Chicago, IL, London, 1990

Laub, Dori; Felman, Shoshanna: *Testimony: Crises of Witnessing in Literature, Psychoanalysis and History*, Routledge, New York, London, 1992

Rawicz, Piotr: Le prophéties de Witkiewicz, *Le Nouvel Observateur*, 22 Juin 1988 (pp. 74–76)

Rosenfeld, Aron, H.: *A Double Dying*, Indiana University Press, Bloomington, 1980

Rudolf, Antony: *Engraved in Flesh*, Menard Press, London, 1996

Sacks, Jonathan: *Crisis and Convenant*, Manchester University Press, 1992

Strauss, Leo: *Persecution and the Art of Writing*, The Free Press, Illinois, 1952

Szondi, Peter: *On Textual Understanding and Other Essays*, Manchester University Press, 1986

Young, James: *The Texture of Memory*, Yale University Press, 1993

Young, James: *Writing and Rewriting the Holocaust*, Indiana University Press, Bloomington, Indianapolis, 1990